Teresa,

Thanks so much for entering this giveaway. I hope you enjoy this book.

All the best,

Mary

POST-ITS
AND POLAROIDS

Snippets and Snapshots from

an Overthought Life

MARY SWAN-BELL

NOTEBOOK
PUBLISHING

First published in 2019 by Notebook Publishing,
20–22 Wenlock Road, London, N1 7GU.

www.notebookpublishing.co

ISBN: 9781913206314

A CIP catalogue record for this book is available from the British Library.

Typeset by Notebook Publishing.

Chloe, Peyton and Lily:
If I never got to be anything but your mom,
that would be enough.
You are the greatest gifts of my life.

AUTHOR'S NOTE

We all have a story to tell.

While our souls know the truth, throughout life, our minds—helped along by the voices of outside influences—distort it. I think it was my girl Glennon Doyle who said: We always tell our truth, but sometimes, it isn't in a healthy way. Sometimes we tell it in the way we eat—or don't eat. Drink too much or smoke or compulsively clean. Sometimes we tell it in a way that looks healthy, such as making sure our kids are dressed perfectly or our house is decorated just so darling. I have tried these techniques in some fashion or other for the past twenty-five years to no avail.

My truth comes out through my fingers. Often in the early morning hours when a sentence forms in my head, and I'm compelled to get up, open my laptop, and let it pour into a Word document.

Pouring out words is cathartic, but it's usually not enough for me. I need to share them. Maybe for validation. Maybe so someone else can say, "Me too." Maybe because my greatest revelations have happened while reading other peoples' words. Maybe because my musings don't feel "real" until someone reads them.

So, as I edit and edit and edit this, I realize that as long as I am alive, my story will evolve. Lessons, experiences, even memories and perceptions of the past. Fluid. Ever-changing. Although this book tells lots of stories, it isn't my whole story. It's the stories of the person I was at lots of different moments. It's an image captured on a Polaroid... a quick note scrawled on a Post-it.

Thanks for reading.

* Some names and identifying facts have been changed.

I love to tell the story of unseen things above,
Of Jesus and His glory, of Jesus and His love;
I love to tell the story, because I know 'tis true,
It satisfies my longings as nothing else would do.

Refrain:
I love to tell the story,
'Twill be my theme in glory,
To tell the old, old story
Of Jesus and His love.

I love to tell the story, more wonderful it seems
Than all the golden fancies of all our golden dreams;
I love to tell the story, it did so much for me,
And that is just the reason I tell it now to thee.

I love to tell the story, 'tis pleasant to repeat,
What seems each time I tell it more wonderfully sweet;
I love to tell the story, for some have never heard
The message of salvation from God's own holy Word.

I love to tell the story, for those who know it best
Seem hungering and thirsting to hear it like the rest;
And when in scenes of glory I sing the new, new song,
'Twill be the old, old story that I have loved so long.

—Arabella Hankey 1866

CAST OF CHARACTERS

Father: Harry Oscar (Dad, Peach, Slim) (1916–2011)

Mother: Catherine Louise (Mom, Nanny) (1931–)

Elizabeth Ann (Beth) (1958–)

Jonathan Leo (Jonny) (1960–)

Christopher James (Chris, Christo, Teeny) (1961–1989)

David Rice (Dave, Tub) (1962–)

Brian Joseph (Bri, Balky) (1964–1997)

Richard Lewis (Rich, Montalban) (1969–)

Mary Catherine (Poo) (1973–)

Husband: Bradley Alan (1974–)

Daughter: Chloe Christina (1994–)

Son: Peyton Joseph (2000–)

Daughter: Lily Catherine (2006–)

INTRODUCTION

FOR A GOOD PART of my life, I felt incomplete. Unworthy. Unlovable. When you don't get loved in the way you feel you need or receive from your mother, arguably, the person who's supposed to love you completely and fully, the person who—in my mind—should know exactly the way you need to be loved, it can make you feel flawed. When I became a mother, I loved my children with a fierce and all-consuming force that threatened to make my heart burst into a million pieces from the first whiff of sweet baby skin.

And yet, I wondered: Why hadn't my mother loved me like this? Why hadn't she snuggled and breathed me in and exploded with pride at my every accomplishment? Was something wrong with me? Wasn't I good enough to evoke this devotion in my mother?

Obviously, it wasn't me. It was her. No, we never had that talk. She never said, "It's not you; it's me." In fact, until I read *The Four Agreements* by Don Miguel Ruiz and realized there was nothing personal in her actions, I had believed that if I'd been a little bit blonder, skinnier, smarter, prettier, more demure... If I'd been a little less opinionated, open-minded, sexy, brash, vulgar... If I'd prayed a little more and drank a little less... If I'd just been more Catholic and less spiritual... If I'd been more like her and less like me, she might have loved me better.

What I didn't understand for a really long time was that even though it didn't feel like love or acceptance, my mom loved me the best she could. She wasn't a warm, fuzzy, let's-talk-about-our-feelings type of mom, but she loved me in her own unique way.

Forty-six years of experience taught me that learning to be a woman in this world is hard. Who am I? How do I act? How do I own my sexuality? What is sex? How do I respond to sexual harassment? What is appropriate and what isn't? In my opinion, and what I taught my daughters: Anything that makes you feel uncomfortable, victimized, attacked, objectified, or icky in any way is inappropriate. In most situations, your gut tells you everything you need to know, including what a person's intentions are. Trust it.

My dad often made inappropriate and sometimes sexually charged comments to women—waitresses, friends, strangers, it didn't matter. While I believe his intent was to be complimentary, playful, and flirtatious, this banter was wrong and made me extremely uncomfortable from a very young age. I felt embarrassed and responsible for protecting the women subjected to these remarks. As a little girl, I tried to catch their gaze, silently apologizing with my eyes. As a woman, I admonished him: "Dad, you can't say shit like that to people!" He ignored me.

Sometimes we have mothers, sisters, grandmothers, and aunts as guides. When we hit the jackpot, our mothers, sisters, grandmothers, and aunts model different ways to be a woman through their actions, behaviors, words, and lessons. How to balance work and parenthood, how to respond to gossip, how to make a pie crust, how to curl your hair, how to treat people, how to do make up, what kind of make-up looks good on you, how to be in a relationship, how to be out of a relationship, what kind of clothes are flattering on you and what aren't, and so many other intricacies of femininity.

Sometimes the mothers, sisters, grandmothers, and aunts we get in the biological lottery don't fill in the blanks for us. More often than not, the women we get are flawed and struggling with their own issues and are unable to love us like we want or need to be loved. Their own issues inhibit their abilities to teach us what we really need to know. When this happens, we can sometimes get stuck trying to make the people we *have* into the people we *need*. But we don't have to do this. We can stop focusing on what's missing and start making lemonade out of those biological lemons. We can choose to accept and let go of who we got in the DNA lottery and start seeking who we actually *do* need.

Maybe it's your best friend's single mom who waitresses all day but still makes time to lie in bed and listen to her daughter talk about her day, calming her and reassuring her that things will get better. Maybe it's your old neighbor, a victim of domestic violence who left her abusive husband, even though it meant moving back in with her parents at 35, with two kids. Maybe it's the cashier who smiles and has a positive attitude every time you see her despite inconsiderate customers who demean her and treat her poorly. Maybe it's the clerk at the post office who tells you how pretty you look in that color and smiles knowingly when you tell her that she made your day. The universe offers us so many teachers, but sometimes we miss these spiritual gifts because we're focused on the people who fall short in the roles we feel they are meant to play.

Raising my own three children, I wanted to be everything to them that I had needed growing up. I wanted to take the good I got from my parents and sift out the bad to make a perfect parenting recipe. However, my own children did not crave the same things I did. On her podcast, "For the Love," author, mom, podcaster and all-around genius, Jen Hatmaker advises, "We have to parent the kids we have, not the kids we were." By trying to be the mom I needed instead of the mom they needed, I was creating a new set of issues that my kids would be working through in therapy. Instead, I had to let them be who they were. Expose them to and let them find people who would serve as their soul teachers. While it may not *take* a village to raise a child, a village definitely helps a child develop into a well-rounded person.

Although I had my parents, my siblings, a "proxy" grandma in the form of my deceased grandmother's best friend, a few neighbors, and my mom's quirky and abundant girlfriends, I didn't feel surrounded by love. My mom tells stories of how she and her sister were shipped off for weeks at a time to stay with her two spinster aunts who treated them like princesses. My own sister talked about how she stayed for weeks at a time with our maternal grandparents (both of whom died within a week of each other when I was in utero) who adored her and felt she was the most wonderful child ever to be born.

I didn't have a village. I didn't even have a very reliable family. People moved out. People moved away. People died.

So, for years, I searched. I searched for belonging in other people's acceptance. I combed others' words for my own worthiness. Along the way, I unearthed long-buried pieces of myself and let go of other parts. Through love, compassion, and empathy, I let go of stories that were no longer true about me—stories that had never been true.

Toni Morrison says, "If there's a book that you want to read, but it hasn't been written yet, then you must write it." I wrote this book to help women do what it took me forty plus years to do: make peace with the past. Heal. Stop trying to make people like me. Stop trying to mold myself into a more acceptable version. Stop looking for the world's confirmation of my worth. Stop trying to make the wrong people into who I need—or want—them to be and allow the right people into my life. The universe will bring us who we need, but sometimes we have to clear out space.

A good story has a beginning, middle, and end. I love to write beginnings. If I could only write introductions, I'd write every day. Endings are a little tougher, but I can write them. I like things to be tied up neatly, preferably with bows—a rare occurrence. But it's the middle where I struggle. Fleshing out the story. Going into detail. The in-the-meantime part. I would prefer intro, yada, yada, yada, end.

So, this is kind of a middle, but it's also kind of the beginning.

In my family of origin, I was the seventh child and only the second girl after five boys in a row. My mom was forty-one during her pregnancy with me, and in her third trimester, her dad succumbed to colon cancer and then her mother died of a heart attack ten days later. I've never talked to her about how difficult it must have been to lose her parents while raising six children and gestating a seventh. She doesn't like to talk about unpleasant things and would often respond to my questions with, "Nice people don't talk about things like this." This is perhaps why I am pathologically drawn to hashing things out. Especially those things that are neither nice nor pleasant.

Obviously, this is my perception, account, and memory of events and situations. Certainly, my mom, siblings, and many others might recall things differently.

Here we go.

I was the baby, and my mom *loves* babies. She is wonderful with babies, and other than the times that she left me as a baby, I'm confident my babyhood was magical. From a childhood development standpoint, I would label myself as insecurely attached. While my mom could be very loving and attentive, at other times, she was cold and distant. I became fearful and unsure, as her behavior was inconsistent. I was very dependent on her, didn't like her to leave, and was terrified each time she left that she wouldn't return. Of course, this fear was intensified by several older brothers who would tell me that she wasn't coming back and a father who screamed and spanked me in frustration when I cried for my mom. The pattern continued until I was about five when I became adept at concealing my feelings. Hiding and crying quietly protected me from my dad's rage and my brothers' ridicule.

But it was also the beginning of a long history of clingy behavior that would plague me—and those I clung to. I needed my mom and felt as if we were two halves of one whole being, and sometimes, she left, leaving me feeling incomplete. When I became upset at her leaving, she was neither compassionate nor empathic to my feelings. She would angrily shove me off, exasperated by my neediness. "Of course I'll be back. I'm only going to a meeting." As an adult, I think she cultivated my neediness only to ultimately feel yoked by it.

She didn't work outside the home but served on the local school board and attended a sewing club with a group of friends. These interests took her out of the house several evenings a month. I see now that she was simply pursuing a little me time or practicing self-care, but my little girl self was filled with dread for those days. Since I'd learned that crying in front of my dad or brothers made the situation infinitely worse, I spent those evenings staring out my bedroom window, willing her car to pull in the driveway. I played games with myself—her car will be among the next ten cars to come down the street—to keep paranoia from overwhelming me when hers wasn't the next car, or the next, or even the next.

Sometimes, I sneaked downstairs and peeked in the family room to see if my dad had fallen asleep in his chair. If he had, I sat at the bottom of the stairs and watched from a first-floor window that gave me a longer view of the street, careful to creep back to my bed if my dad stirred. Some nights, I spent three or four hours waiting by the window before my mom finally arrived at ten or eleven p.m. Upon seeing her car, I was so relieved that I could go to bed and sleep soundly.

When I went to elementary school, I desperately missed my mom and was extremely worried that something would happen to her while I was gone during the day. I was the poster child for separation anxiety. I finally felt secure enough to go to school without crying all day in second grade. The next year, my mom decided to homeschool me.

Homeschooling was very rare in the late 70s, and I feared other peoples' opinions. I never wanted to stand out or draw attention to myself, and this did exactly that. I feared people would think I was weird, a freak, if they knew. In my home, few things mattered more than what other people thought. So rather than tell people what I felt was an embarrassing story, I crafted elaborate lies about a private academy where I attended school. I had a lofty imagination but minimal deception skills, so I became an expert listener. I carefully redirected conversations away from my own life, which felt embarrassing, and back to others' seemingly more normal lives. Thankfully, most people would rather talk about themselves than listen anyway, so I skated by without anyone learning about my freakish secret.

During my years of homeschooling, we spent a lot of time at our very strict, conservative, traditional Catholic church. To my knowledge, the priest didn't molest the altar boys, but he did hate Jews. He celebrated the Mass in Latin, and I never understood the words we repeated week in and week out. In fact, the first time I heard the

Mass performed in English, I was completely intrigued—though not enough to keep attending Catholic Church—to finally understand all those rote phrases. "In nomine Patris et Filii et Spiritus Sancti" meant nothing to me, but "In the name of the Father and the Son and the Holy Spirit" did.

One of the off-brand subjects we studied in our home school was Latin. My mom also taught three other children who attended our church. The purpose of studying Latin was to understand the Mass, which I never did, but it proved helpful later when my children studied Latin and Greek root words in their own English programs.

During this period of non-separation of church and school: We went to church once a week and for every holy day. You may be aware, if you are or were Catholic, that Catholicism boasts lots of holy days and feast days. On St. Patrick's Day, we wore green but went to church instead of the bar. On the feast of the Assumption, we celebrated Mary, the mother of Christ, being whisked body and all into heaven. The whole month of May was about Mary, in fact, culminating in a May crowning, during which, one lucky child was chosen to lead the procession to adorn the statue Mary's head with a crown of flowers. I was never picked, which made me feel relieved and overlooked at the same time.

All Saints' Day was my personal favorite. I'm not sure how this was explained to me, but in my nine-year-old mind, here was the gist: Saying a certain number of specific prayers allowed you to release souls from purgatory and free them to go to heaven. Purgatory, for those unfamiliar with these mythical places, is where souls go in the meantime after death. No one, according to the Roman Catholic Church, is good enough to go straight to heaven, so they have to spend some time in this place working off their sins or waiting for good little girls to pray them out on November 1.

This concept felt extremely empowering, and I wore my knees out on the pleather-covered wooden plank known as a kneeler, praying souls into heaven. Mostly, I focused on the babies in Limbo. Limbo was the place where poor unbaptized babies went, as they were born with original sin on their souls, their innocent little selves complicit in Eve's transgression. This felt like a monumental miscarriage of justice. In fact, it's probably the reason why stories of people being framed for something they didn't do still trigger me.

Another way of winning favor with the fire and brimstone God of the Catholic Church was through "offering up" your sacrifice and suffering. Like penance— the practice of saying a priest-assigned number of Our Fathers or Hail Marys to make restitution for lying or having impure thoughts or swearing or whatever sins you'd confessed—you could offer painful experiences up for heavenly bonus points. For example, I have an aversion to wool, but wore a very itchy uncomfortable wool skirt that my mother made for me every week. I then "offered up" my discomfort for souls in purgatory. Similarly, I inflicted my own suffering by holding my urine as long as possible before using the bathroom. This actually resulted in recurrent bladder infections, no more bubble baths, and a stern lecture about my stupidity.

When I weighed the number of babies who made it into heaven at the expense of my bladder, it still seemed worthwhile. Still, I didn't do it anymore. Later, when I dabbled in a different flavor of Christianity, the concept of not "earning" God's love and grace seemed like smoke and mirrors.

Despite spending nearly all day every day with her, I clung desperately to my mom. When she decided to send me back to public school—in eighth grade—it felt like betrayal and culture shock. My sister told me later that she had encouraged my mom to send me back to school in eighth grade as she'd felt this preparatory year would help me adjust better to high school the next year. While her intentions were good and genuine, eighth grade was no fucking picnic.

I don't remember anything I learned during the years of homeschooling, but my mother proudly reiterates the story of her first conference with my eighth grade English teacher when he supposedly said, "I don't know what I am going to teach her. She already knows everything." That being the case, I entered eighth grade on an intellectual par with other kids. Socially, however, I interacted at a second grade level.

One of my few saving graces was that I was society's definition of attractive, and years of gymnastics classes meant that I could do flips, which made me both an oddity and an interest. Plus, thanks to a shopping trip to the nearest big city—Cleveland—with my dad, I had some semi-fashionable (but definitely expensive) clothing. My dad firmly believed that an item's coolness ratio was determined by its price tag. I was scared and insecure and felt incapable and ill-equipped for this adventure. I cried nonstop for about a month. I missed my mom, but it wasn't socially acceptable to miss your mother in eighth grade, so I made up reasons for why I cried every day. I can't remember any of them. At the same time, I was so angry with her for abandoning me to this scary and foreign situation. I hated and missed and needed and worried about her. I felt misunderstood, alone, and my parents and brothers chided me to grow up and stop acting like a baby. My sister, who had pushed for my reintegration, was not available to offer support. She was busy with her own life, nursing career, three small children, and another on the way.

What I realized after being thrust into public school was that there was a great big world outside of our home school in the basement. And that world was filled with boys and cigarettes and alcohol and drugs. Similarly, I quickly realized that all I had to do was avoid embarrassing my mother, get good grades, smile, be polite, and wipe my eyeliner off on the bus on my way home from school—I wasn't allowed to wear makeup until I was sixteen—and I could fully partake in boys, cigarettes, alcohol, and drugs.

I always felt a sense of lacking in my relationship with my mother but couldn't quite put my finger on what was lacking. In hindsight, I think I longed for a depth of physical and emotional intimacy that she wasn't capable of giving. She wasn't much of a hugger, no one really said, "I love you," and meaningful and heartfelt conversations were extremely rare. She usually hugged me awkwardly before shoving me away. After a very young age, I couldn't curl up in her lap and snuggle with her. I couldn't tell her what I was sad about or afraid of or worrying over, which was always something as I was a particularly anxious child. My sister recalled an instance from her own childhood when she approached our mom crying and asserting her fear that our mother would die, and that our mother huffed in response, "I'm not going to die. That's the stupidest thing I've ever heard." My mother's main form of communication was jokes, criticism, and sarcasm but never the real deep and honest communication that I longed for.

Although I didn't realize it for many years, now I see that I sought out the "mom" qualities I wanted in other people. My dad, for instance, despite our rocky beginnings, became one of my most trusted confidants, and in later years, made me feel unconditionally loved and accepted.

While I am no parenting expert, I fully believe that if you are willing to own your flaws and apologize to your children when you make mistakes, your children will grow up to love and forgive you and to accept the mistakes you made parenting them as foibles of your own humanity. I freely forgave my dad for his shortcomings because he loved me fully, took responsibility for his mistakes, and asked for forgiveness. If we could practice that authenticity and accountability in all of our relationships, we'd likely feel significantly less animosity and pain.

My teenage years were the worst with my mother, as many teen girls and mothers of teen girls can probably relate. We are very different. Physically. Mentally.

Emotionally. Where she was a bundle of high-strung neurotic energy, I could lie in bed watching Netflix for hours. I work—pathologically at times—on self-improvement, and she points out flaws in others while avoiding acknowledging any of her own. I love deep introspective conversations, and she prefers gossip and jokes. We are polar opposites, and that polarity caused multiple explosions during my teen years.

Although our family home was just around the corner from my mom's childhood home, we went to a large inner-city high school, not the small Catholic school my mom and her siblings had attended. Unlike my mom, I had been deprived from normal society for so long that by the time I was fully acclimated—about halfway through eighth grade—I wanted to fully engage in every devious aspect of teenage debauchery. I wanted to drink and smoke and do "impure" things with boys. I wanted to finally have something juicy to tell the priest on the other side of the screen... something that made my Hail Marys worthwhile.

In hindsight, I think a lot about the phrase, "What we fear we manifest," and I wonder if I became the exact person my mom was trying to prevent or maybe protect me from becoming with the homeschooling and modest dresses and short haircuts. It felt like she was trying desperately to make me into a mini version of her, but my rebel spirit couldn't be completely broken.

By the time I hit my partying apex and found myself pregnant at twenty, she had pretty much washed her hands of me. When I told her I was pregnant, she had mixed reactions.

"How could you be so stupid?"

"I thought you were on the pill?"

And then finally, she said, "Well, getting pregnant isn't the worst thing that ever happened to a person."

Still, she asked me to move out.

When I became a mother myself, my mom issues kicked in full force.

Most people are aware of the sentiment: When the student is ready, the teacher appears. My teachers started showing up long before I was prepared for the lessons. However, nothing makes a person wake up and pay attention—at least people with a shred or two of self-awareness—than being responsible for another life. I never wanted my future baby to feel insecure or unloved or unworthy or any negative emotion I'd endured for one second, but in order to be any good to anyone else, you have to be good to yourself. Take the advice flight attendants offer before take-off, "Put your own oxygen mask on before you attempt to help others." If you don't address your own issues, you will pass them and a whole host of new ones on.

I'll always be a work in progress. The stories in this book are my offering to those who have felt misunderstood. To the person who felt that no one really got them. To the person who felt they may have been switched at birth because they never truly belonged in their family. To anyone who thought they needed a different mom than the one they got. You belong. Someone gets you—I promise. Maybe you've just been looking in the wrong places for understanding.

CHAPTER 1:
TELL YOUR STORY;
HEAL YOUR SOUL

"You own everything that happened to you. Tell your stories. If people wanted you to write warmly about them, they should have behaved better."

—*Anne Lamott*

M Y MOTHER WAS AN English teacher for a few years before she became a full-time wife and mother. However, she embodied the Catholic school teacher archetype for the rest of her life. She corrected our speech from the moment we could say "Dada," and if my siblings and I share one common trait, it's excellent grammar.

However, she was not particularly moved by those who used her beloved English language in a creative way. My brother, a writer and playwright, wrote dark, moving pieces. Stuff that kept you up at night and questioning everything about your life and family and choices. My mother would read these pieces, shrug, and with a sour expression say, "I don't know why he can't write anything happy." Most writers write what they know, and we didn't always know happy. However, my mom did such a good job of painting a picture of the cheerful life she wanted, that she wouldn't admit our actual life didn't really look like that picture.

When I started writing, naturally, as a good little wanting-acceptance-and-approval girl, I wrote happy, funny things. My mom loves a good joke, so my goal was to make people laugh. I rarely wrote about things that bothered me, but if I did, it was only with a funny spin on them. We could talk about my dad beating us or losing his temper if it ended in a punchline. My freshman year in college, I read Anne Lamott's *Bird by Bird*, and it completely changed my course as a writer and a person.

The title, *Bird by Bird*, comes from a story Anne Lamott tells about her teenaged brother who was completely overwhelmed and frustrated by a report he'd been assigned to write on birds. Her dad calmly encouraged him not to be undone by the enormity of the report but instead to take it "bird by bird."

Anne Lamott encourages her writing students to share their unedited truth, their "shitty first drafts." Her advice became my mantra: "You own everything that happened to you. Tell your stories. If people wanted you to write warmly about them, they should have behaved better." Over the next few years, I alienated a few people by sharing my unedited stories.

From Lamott's wisdom and teaching, I learned to appreciate "shitty first drafts," and how important it is to "just fucking write it down," as she encourages aspiring or blocked writers. In fact, the advice I've heard repeated over and over from loads of successful authors and even a divine intervention, which I'll tell you about in a minute, is simply, "Write."

Several years ago, I started writing a book about my family experiences, a memoir of sorts. Many days when I sat down to write, my fingers flew across the keys, and the words flowed out of me as if they were coming from a divine source. In fact, at the time, I was completely caught up in a Christian church and believed they *were* coming from a divine source. I wrote and wrote and wrote. Sometimes, when I re-read what I had written, the words seemed foreign, and I had no recollection of writing them. I was in a zone, and this solidified my belief that these words originated from a divine source.

I told my story from childhood to the present bluntly and unabashedly. The writing was so poignant in some passages that it didn't seem possible it came from my head. Painstakingly, I edited it and crafted a book proposal based on the best advice of Linda Sivertsen and Danielle LaPorte's *My Big Beautiful Book Plan*. Crossing tasks off rapidly, I now had to find an agent and a publisher, and I would make my dreams come true ahead of schedule.

Then my computer tragically died, and the 39,000 words that I hadn't thought to back up anywhere were lost forever. I was completely devastated. Foolishly, I'd thought, "It's 2015, I don't need to back it up anywhere. That shit doesn't happen anymore." In fact, that shit does still happen. It does. It did.

Losing the book that had seemed like my purpose for so long, I felt defeated, let down, depressed, and worthless. I believed that those words were the best I had to offer, and they were gone. So much work... gone. So many words... lost.

As often is my M.O., I immediately began drawing conclusions:

This book was not meant to be published.

I was only supposed to write that stuff to help me process it.

No one was meant to read my words.

That book couldn't be published; it would have been too hurtful to my family of origin.

I'm not supposed to be a writer. That is not my purpose after all.

This was my pattern for years. Upon encountering an obstacle, I saw a sign and assumed that I'd misinterpreted my divine guidance and immediately turned around and headed in a different direction. When you're on the right path, things come easily, and doors fly open for you. Right? No. That hardly ever happens.

A few years ago, upon hitting a roadblock and immediately deciding I'd misinterpreted the signs and was headed the wrong way, I got this bit of advice: Maybe it isn't a roadblock. Maybe it's a detour. Or maybe you're just supposed to move this obstacle and keep going. Another of my favorite motivational authors and speakers, Rachel Hollis, inspires her tribe of loyal followers by saying, "Maybe you were given this mountain to show others it can be moved." I hadn't met her work yet, but this advice resonated deeply in me.

Wait. So perhaps I am going the right way, and instead of finding a new goal, a new path, a new purpose, I actually need to go *around* this fallen tree or washed out bridge or broken computer and keep going. Keep. Going. What a revelation.

Looking back through my life, I saw a distinct pattern of times interpreting hardships as signs that I was on the wrong path when that might not have been the case at all. Rather than question every decision I'd ever made in my life and getting stuck in a giant spin cycle of regret, I decided that from that moment forward, I would break the pattern of going home when the going got tough.

Initially, when it seemed writing a book was a giant bust, I threw myself into my happy and fulfilling roles of mom, wife, daughter, encourager, supporter, and friend. If this is my purpose, this is more than enough. I took my usual route and hit the library to stock up on books to help me re-charge my life, live with purpose, pursue a simple life, and live with passion. I started doing yoga and meditating daily to clear my mind, improve my focus, and be a better, stronger version of myself.

No book? Okay, I will run toward the next best thing—pathological self-improvement. Full. Speed. Ahead. That doesn't work? Okay, well, then I will try this. No? Okay, well, I will do that. That's not working? Okay, then... and so on. But I never seemed to really reach a goal because whenever I hit a stumbling block, I turned and walked or often ran a different way. My kids and husband jokingly call me Sidetrack Sally, but during this transition, it became abundantly clear that this habit could be destructive.

Through all of my yoga, meditation, prayer, reading, and self-reflection, something tugged at my heart. Every book, TED Talk, and podcast reinforced the same message: Write. Most writers will tell you that they don't necessarily choose to write, but I mostly thought that sounded like bullshit. Yet, I find that I can't make sense of the world and my place in it without writing about it.

I listened to the still small voice which patiently whispered, "Write." I drew diagrams and life summaries, realizing all the while what the answer would be: Write. Finally, one night, as I struggled to get comfortable in the twelve inches of space and half a sheet allowing my eight-year-old to share the bed had afforded me, I prayed, "God, please help me to be quiet and hear what you want to say to me." The answer resonated with thundering clarity in my soul: Write. In fact, the clairaudience was so jarring and surreal that I jumped—waking my tiny girl and affording me a better sleeping spot. Write.

But... I already did. I had tried and was pretty convinced that the best writing I was capable of had been contained in those 39,000 words that were lost forever in cyber-hell. Wasn't it?

Maybe those 39,000 words were a shitty first draft. Maybe they were 39,000 deeply personal and self-indulgent words that I had to slog through in order to write anything worthwhile. Well, worthwhile for anything other than my own therapy. Maybe.

Then there was this other thing...

I've been writing the same story for more than twenty years in my head, in poems, essays, and blogs. If I don't write this story, then what the heck am I going to write? I've heard many different expressions of this same notion: We all only have one story to tell, and everything will just be some different version, some varying aspect of the same core narrative.

My core narrative was the dark memories impressed on my soul during my childhood and adolescence. I write to process pain and ultimately to heal the hurting. A few months after my dad died, I had a minor mental breakdown. For a few months, I struggled to get out of bed and couldn't stop crying. My doctor diagnosed mild depression and perhaps a teensy bit of bipolar II, so she prescribed an anti-depressant/mood stabilizer. She assured me I wouldn't need it forever but promised it would help me through this valley. I felt really good for about three months on the medication. My moods were stable for the first time in my life, and I was pretty happy. Actually happy is a stretch. I was calm and even. I didn't have mood swings because I only experienced one mood.

During those three months, however, I did not write one word. Probably because I am not really a calm, even person. In fact, I have always been kind of moody, but age afforded me the wisdom and ability to manage, work with, and ultimately embrace my mood swings. I get a ton of stuff accomplished during my mildly manic episodes, and I write, cry, meditate, and read my way through dark places. Realizing this wasn't the right path for me, I took myself off the medication—which isn't advised, and I don't recommend—and let myself be sad for a while. Then I wrote about it.

Through this process, some things became very clear: I don't write because I'm driven for publication, and being published doesn't make me more or less of a writer. I write from an inner drive to figure things out, to wrap my head around my feelings, and sometimes to heal my spirit. I don't usually write about happy stuff because I don't feel the need to process the happy. Instead, I ruminate on the sad, hard stuff that muddies up my journey to the happily ever after. In fact, I feel a slight compulsion to write about sadness lest it sneak up when I'm not paying attention and steal my joy. I like to keep the darkness out in front of me in order to keep an eye on it.

In one of my favorite movies, *The Divine Secrets of the Ya-Ya Sisterhood*, a touching scene takes place between Vivianne Walker Abbott (Ellen Burstyn) and her future son-in-law Connor McGill (Angus Macfadyen). Connor is explaining to his future mother-in-law what he believes to be his fiancée, Sidda's (Sandra Bullock), irrational fear that the bottom is always about to fall out. Brené Brown would later coin this phenomenon of waiting for the other shoe to drop as "foreboding joy." Vivi, in her molasses-y drawl, meets Connor's frustration with, "You know why she thinks that, don't ya, honey? Because it did. It always did."

If you ask my six siblings to tell our family's story, they'd tell six very different ones. Four, actually. Two didn't live to tell the story. The soundtrack of their stories would likely be different as well, but Jim Reeves, Cristy Lane, and Hank Williams—my dad's music—would feature prominently. Sprinkle in CCR, Led Zeppelin, The Doors, and America. Bruce Springsteen's anthems would bolster young egos who did too many drugs, punched holes in walls, and crept down the back steps with baseball bats to settle scores. Neil Young would sorrowfully mourn four dead in Ohio, while we ultimately would mourn two. And I would belt out, "Stroke me," with Billy Squier, my eight-year-old self completely unaware of the sexual innuendo. Music served each of us in different ways. It was my escape. I could put on big black headphones and let Billy's voice drown out the crying, yelling, screaming, and swearing. Although we share parents, DNA, parts of the story, some of the ups, most of the tragedies, and the experience of growing up in the same house, I think our strongest common bond is heartbreak. We all experienced and processed it differently. Some of our stories run parallel and some intersect. I'm going to do my best to tell my story without sharing too much of my siblings'. Except my dead brothers'; I'm going to tell some of their stories... the ones that intermingle and help form parts of mine.

Naturally, I'll start in one of the darkest places. You know, keep it up front.

Sunday, February 5, 1989. It was five days after my sixteenth birthday, and I woke late, eleven a.m. or so. My mom came into my room, whispering, "Come downstairs when you're ready; I need to talk to you about something."

Instantly the world felt... off. Gut feelings can be distinct—I'm in danger, that person is bad, someone is lying, this place isn't safe. Or they can be vague—Something is not quite right. We all have them. My dad encouraged me to rely on mine. Once, when I was nine, my gut feeling sent me running to a pay phone when a gymnastics coach who was visiting our gym from another facility tried to grab me after I'd repeatedly turned down his offers for shopping, candy, toys, and a stuffed animal. My gut said, "You are not safe." Later, my mom's conversation with the other coaches confirmed my feelings, and he was removed on the spot. While it was one of the only times my feelings were validated as a little girl, it was enough. Now, this time, my gut wasn't swirling in that about-to-be-caught-in-a-lie anxiety often experienced by rebellious teenagers. It wasn't signaling danger. This felt different. My gut indicated that after I walked down those stairs, my life would exist in two parts: Before February 5th, 1989, and after. Heavy with anticipation, I trudged reluctantly down the stairs.

My siblings and I joke that our mother has a "voice." My sister would call and say, "Mom called this morning. She had the voice." My brother periodically texts, "Mom left me a voicemail. She had the voice. Did someone die?" I'm not sure if we were aware of the voice before that day, but we're all well aware of it now.

The voice is shaky but not tearful. Strained, as if every muscle in her body is tensing from the effort of pushing air from her lungs through her throat to tickle her vocal cords in a barely audible way, and finally slithering through the tight slit of her mouth to say—on that particular snowy morning—"Chris is dead."

She said it so quietly that I didn't react at all, simply stared at her in disbelief. I sat very still and then shook my head, letting the sounds bang around in there for a few seconds, willing them to form different words. Chris is not dead. Chris can't be dead. Who is dead? "No." I responded defiantly. "Do you mean Dad is dead?" My mom shook her head. I felt drunk or like I was in a nightmare I couldn't wake up from. She was saying these words, but they couldn't possibly be true. My sister sat a few feet away at the other end of the church bench in our dining room. I looked down at her, waiting for some sign that this wasn't really happening. I willed her to shake her head or give me a "Mom's lost it" sign. Instead, she quietly sobbed and nodded. I thought about lying down and curling up in a ball. Maybe if I put my feet against one end of the slippery church bench and propelled myself to the other like I used to do when I was very little, I could make this stop. Maybe physical movement would jar me out of this nightmare.

How? Where? When? Why? What???? I was immediately a journalist. But few of my questions could be answered. Where? In a locked bathroom stall at work. Who? Chris. Yes, but did someone kill him? We don't know. How? We don't know. Why? We don't know.

The next days were filled with questions. Over the course of twenty-nine years, some of those would be answered, though never fully. Some painfully. Some shockingly. Some not at all.

Most people have a hero. A person they admire. Someone who makes you want to be better, be fearless, be the best version of yourself.

For me, that person was my brother Chris. For some of the following reasons:

- He was fearless.
- He was the first and, for a long time, the only person ever to tell me he loved me. The Swans didn't say I love you; you were just supposed to know. I felt special and set apart that my brother told me he loved me.
- He took me to Cedar Point with lifts in my shoes so I was tall enough to ride every roller coaster.
- He taught me to drive. Automatic and standard, though I never really got the whole clutch/gas connection.
- He bought me a trampoline so I could practice gymnastics and maybe someday be as good of a gymnast as he was.

- He drove my best friend and me to cheerleading practice our freshman year of high school in his Corvette and laughed as our friends whispered and blushed and gushed, "Who's that?"
- He made me drive that stupid Corvette on the highway when I didn't even have a permit. "I'm scared!" I screamed, and he joked, "You should be—you're going twenty-five on the highway. It's a Corvette! Put your foot on the gas before you get us killed!"
- He took my best friend and I to see INXS, my favorite band, and bought us wine coolers.
- He dated beautiful, smart, accomplished women, who became my beloved sisters and trusted friends.
- He was the coolest person I knew.
- He jumped out of airplanes and promised me that when I was sixteen, he would take me skydiving.

He. Was. Perfect. He was my idea of what a man should be. I loved him so much; it didn't seem fathomable that he could die. He was larger than life. Invincible. Too good to be true. In fact, that was true: He was all of those things I believed him to be, but he had another side I knew nothing about.

Stories compiled over the years showed a different side of him. Stories from siblings, friends, and someone who dated him piled up and revealed a person very different from the one who lived on in my heart.

My brother Chris was charming, charismatic, and a daredevil. He was also a drug addict. He used morphine, heroin, cocaine, and PCP. He also sold drugs. He owned twenty plus rental houses in the area we lived. He was "flipping" properties before that was a thing. Buying, fixing up, and renting properties. Building an empire. Networking. All while working midnights as a nurse at the Cleveland Clinic and pursuing an MBA. He was a star.

Unfortunately, his empire was built on a shaky foundation. He owed lots of people money. His houses were behind on taxes. His empire was about to come crashing down, but before he was forced to deal with that, he died on a cold bathroom floor in one of the most prestigious hospitals in the world. I never jumped out of an airplane, nor did I ever have the desire. I'm not sure if his death was intentional or accidental, and that's one question that will likely never be answered, but it stopped mattering a long time ago.

The last time I saw him, he gave me a card congratulating me for getting my driver's license and reminding me to go at least the speed limit on the highway. He hugged me and kissed me and told me he loved me. I never saw him alive again.

Despite the stories of who other people thought he was, he will always be the big brother I adored and admired. I see glimpses of him in my kids sometimes and wish they could have met him. My oldest daughter Chloe has his drive and determination. She pushes herself harder than anyone I know. My son Peyton has his charm, his feet, those crazy hitchhiker thumbs, and the same curls around his ears. Like his uncle, Peyton has an adventurous spirit and the ability to make me smile regardless of the circumstances. He is the only other man who shares my DNA that I have loved with such fierce abandon. And my youngest daughter Lily is fearless. She does flips off the end of the couch and makes my heart stop on a regular basis.

Any family that's ever lost an important member knows how devastating it can be. Chris' death upended our family in a way that no one was prepared to weather, and no one could ever repair. Despite what controversies might have gone on within our walls, from the outside, few people would have suspected things were less than perfect in the Swan house. Eight years later, another brother's death would knock down what was left of that perfect façade.

So, I know dark. I can write about it. But I learned as years went on that I didn't have to be what Elizabeth Gilbert so eloquently describes as a "tortured artist." In fact, writing and ruminating and rehashing the same shit over and over no longer served me and kept me stuck in an old pattern with old people in an old story that was no longer mine.

So I tried writing from this good, happy place that's my life now, and as it turns out: I can write happy too. In fact, happiness multiplies when I write about it. Maybe all those years writing about the sad was actually multiplying that, but I'm not going to go there and beat myself up. As Gretchen Rubin says, "Onward and upward!"

Everyone can benefit from telling their stories. To a therapist. To a friend. To your husband. Or maybe in a book. I love to read memoirs. I love to read peoples' stories whether they are of overcoming a hardship or just dealing with life. Hearing other peoples' stories and perspectives is inspiring.

We can all write and re-write our own stories through truth, vulnerability, and bravely and authentically being exactly who we are. That's not a bad story. Thanks, Annie, for reminding me that shitty first drafts are okay. In fact, they're more than okay. They're essential.

CHAPTER 2:
AS IT TURNS OUT,
FOOD IS NOT LOVE

"If we think our job here on earth is to fix ourselves, we will keep looking for the broken places. If we believe our job is to be kind, we will keep lavishing love on ourselves."
—*Geneen Roth*

W E'RE TAUGHT THAT WE have to learn history in order to avoid repeating mistakes of the past. So, in order to become the person I wanted to be, I had to take a long hard look at how I became the person I was. Over the course of my life, female relationships have broken, mended, and ultimately helped to shape me into who I am. Unfortunately, some of the relationships of my formative years that "should" have been the closest, safest, and most inspiring were some of the most dangerous, fraught with passive-aggressiveness, jealousy, contempt, criticism, favoritism, and lots of other negative-isms.

My relationship with my mom was mostly passive-aggressive, critical, and superficial. My relationship with my sister was often dependable, but also unpredictable. I could count on her to save me from imminent danger or to take me to get birth control, but when it came to hashing out some of the crazy stuff that went on in our family, it didn't seem that we would be allies. My relationship with my mother-in-law started out great, but ultimately was crushed under the heavy pressure of my unrealistic expectations. Fortunately, all of these relationships taught me valuable, if sometimes painful, lessons about the type of mother, sister, friend, and woman I aspired to be. And it all started with food.

One of the greatest struggles of my life has been my weight. My mom and sister are thin. Twiggy thin. Heroin-chic. Skin and bones. Fashionably thin. Really physically tiny women. My sister acknowledged to me before that she struggled with disordered eating in her past, but as far as I know, my mother has never had the same insight. My sister hasn't always been rail-thin, but as a teenager, she rebelled against my mother by restricting food and has kept her weight tightly controlled ever since. Anyway, the two of them tip the scales at about fifty pounds less than me. I weigh 145—a bit above average for my slightly over five-foot frame. They said, "You're not shaped like us. You're big boned." I'm not really big boned.

For my height—according to my physician and the "ideal weight charts" Google showed me—I fluctuate between the high end of normal and the low end of overweight. So, it is actually a normal weight. I'm not skinny. I'm not obese. Most people probably wouldn't even describe me as plump, chubby, chunky, or any of the euphemisms used to describe women who don't fit into society's skinny mold. Thick. That's one I heard recently. Or slim thick, which Urban Dictionary defines as a thin girl with ample booty and breasts. Good grief.

My husband says I'm curvy, which is an adjective I like. Especially how he says it with a sparkle in his eye and smirk playing on his lips. Especially after all the years I spent trying to live up to my mother's ideal of beauty: Bone-thin, platinum blonde, bright lips.

Years ago, a video circulated on social media in which women described themselves to a police sketch artist. The artist drew a portrait from their descriptions. Then strangers spent a few moments with the same women and offered their descriptions to the artist. Again, he sketched their portraits, but this time from the strangers' descriptions. When they compared the sketches, the differences are startling. The women portrayed are visibly moved when they glimpse the image others see versus the image they feel they project to the world. Many of us probably see a reflection that is not necessarily the same image others see when they look at us.

When I was about seven or eight, my brothers called me "Sparrow Butt"—an indication of my skinny little frame. They teased me, "No boys are ever gonna like you."

At this point in life, my mother's calling was to feed me. Any food I remotely liked, she bought in bulk to keep me eating... to fatten me up, she says now. Between ages three and four, I mostly survived on cheese doodles and Tang—the grotesquely sweet fake orange predecessor to Sunny Delight. My mother told this story for years, complaining about what a difficult and defiant child I'd been. The last time she told the story—referencing my own strong-willed child as not falling far from her defiant mother tree—I snapped back, "I was a literal baby. I could only eat what you gave me. Why did you keep giving me cheese doodles and Tang?" She looked at me as if I'd asked her why she went to confession instead of therapy or why it was that she could empathize with other people's children but not her own. She looked at me like not feeding a child whatever it wanted to eat was completely absurd. From then on, she prefaced the story with, "She hates when I tell this story..."

For most of my childhood, I wore slim clothes that hung off me. In the late 1970's when tight Jordache and Gloria Vanderbilt jeans were the trend, I wore Levi's that hung pathetically from my pointy hip bones. After five sons, my nearly fifty-year-old mom didn't know much about what was fashionable for a young girl. I could either dress like her—a fashionable Catholic school marm—or I could dress like my brothers. Naturally, I chose to dress like them.

I used to lie on the floor and contort myself into shapes, mimicking the 1970's Black Velvet advertisement. The model lay provocatively on her side, slim waist, curved hip, platinum blonde hair, red lips, and sexy black dress. I looked like a 2 x 4. Straight. I could not wait to have hips.

For six years as a competitive gymnast, my coach told me I was too tall ever to be a good gymnast. She explained that tumbling would naturally be more difficult for me since I had such long legs. Her statements made me feel increasingly self-conscious of my skinny, *long* limbs and big feet.

Describing my thirteen-year-old self to a police sketch artist would likely have resulted in a portrait that looked like Olive Oyl or Alice the Goon. The person I saw in the mirror was tall, gangly, and awkward. I was five feet tall, weighed eighty pounds and wore (still wear) a size six shoe. I once said something about my long legs to my future husband, who giggled and said, "Baby, you do not have long legs."

While I was far from an elite gymnast, I spent several hours a week in classes and training and was in good physical shape. As the years passed, I was no longer bony, but strong and lean. When tumbling turned into trying to turn boys' heads, intense training morphed into long lazy phone calls. I gained weight very quickly, blowing up from eighty to a hundred pounds in a few short months. Stretch marks that my husband would later refer to as "tiger stripes" split the soft skin on my hips and breasts, marking this transition. My butt lost its sparrow-like tendencies and became rather round. So round, in fact, that a few years later, when I tried on my prom dress for my mom, she asked if I'd be wearing a girdle.

"A girdle? Why? Do you think my stomach sticks out?"

She responded, "No, but your rear end sure does."

Practically overnight, baby got back. My mother shifted from begging and pleading with me to eat because I needed some meat on my bones to questioning, "Are you sure you want to eat that? You probably don't need another one of those. Do you want ice cream *and* chips?" And so forth.

While my sense of size remains warped—I think I am taller than I really am—years of criticism made me pretty sure of my girth. Comments such as, "You don't have the eating habits of a thin person," and eye-rolling sent the message to my brain that my weight was unacceptable. I went on my first diet in eighth grade, shortly after quitting gymnastics and ballooning to one hundred pounds.

When I had my first boyfriend, we spent a lot of time eating, watching movies, and falling in young love. I gained more weight, climbing up the scale to about 120. When our relationship ended, he chided that no one else would date me because my ass was so big. What a conundrum. My brothers told me boys wouldn't like me when I had no ass. The boy I was head over heels in love with told me that no one would like me because I had such a big ass. Even at seventeen, I found that puzzling.

Over the years, I realized that men and women of varying ages and cultures appreciate a big ass, but at the time, I felt hurt and sad. If I'd described myself to a police sketch artist then, the resulting portrait would probably look something like Miss Piggy. I was 5'3" and weighed 125 pounds. Too fat.

As a fully grown adult woman, my thinnest ever frame was when I got married. I weighed about a hundred pounds. At my last dress fitting, the short, plump, sixtyish, Italian seamstress gripped my hipbones aggressively and shook me saying, "Eat something, sweetheart. You lose another pound, your dress gonna fall off you when you walk down the aisle."

Even at a hundred pounds, it didn't seem that I was skinny enough to be considered "pretty" by my mom. On my wedding day, I don't remember her even saying, "You look nice." My husband and nearly everyone else at the wedding complimented me. A dear friend's mom told me that I looked like a real, live Barbie doll, which made my whole day. And while I felt like a princess, it stung that my own mother didn't offer any kind words.

My weight was a huge and consistent factor for most of my life. One of my mom's weapons of choice was cookies, prompting me to invoke the mantra, "Cookies, not love." In childhood though, cookies felt like love. My mom spoke the love language of feeding people. She made chicken noodle soup for the sick. She made a big roast or some kind of meat for special occasions and big achievements. She made each of us our favorite meal *and* favorite cake for our birthdays.

That's not a bad thing, and it was her way to show love through food. In fact, lots of moms and other people show affection by cooking and baking for their loved ones. Sometimes, I shower my kids with food love too. Our Christmas traditions include baking and decorating cookies. We celebrate birthdays with cakes, and sometimes, I surprise them with their favorite treats for special occasions, like Monday. However, my mother also weaponized food to control, belittle, and shame us. Some people use their fists, a paddle, a backhand, or a belt, my mom used sharp words and chocolate chips. She would make a delicious cake and then snidely remark, "Ohhhh, you're having *another* piece of cake?" "Do you really think you need another helping of potatoes?" "I guess I'll have to make more cookies since you devoured those." And her favorite: "You really don't have the eating habits of a thin person."

My dad often suffered more than I did in the food department. He really couldn't win. If she made a cake and he didn't eat it, she was offended, packed it up, took it to a friend, and gave him the silent treatment. If she made something that he liked and did eat, she then shamed him about his weight. My dad liked to eat and to make his wife happy, so he played along good naturedly most of the time. Me, I was so hungry for her love that however she served it, I greedily ate it up.

The only person ever to beat my mom at this game was my sister. The merits of winning that battle are debatable though. One old photo album contains a few pictures of my sister as a teenager when she was not extremely thin. My mom has gleefully referred to this brief period as her "fat phase," and pointed out with great delight her eldest daughter's "big moon face," or snarked that her face was as "round as a dinner plate."

Once, as she was going on about this, I countered, "She was not fat. She looks good. Healthy." After a huge eye roll and disparaging gasp, she admonished, "I BET SHE WEIGHED 112 POUNDS!" At the time, I was tipping the scales at a whopping 112 pounds, so I said, "That's what I weigh. Do you think I have a big moon face?" "No," she said, "but you are much bigger boned than we are." Again, I don't know if you know what a person who is 5'3" and 112 pounds looks like, but big-boned isn't a phrase most people would use to describe them. Unfortunately, after my sister got skinny, my mom's recourse was to criticize her for *not* eating. She called her "anexoric"; mocking her controlled eating and my dad's mispronunciation of anorexic, a dual-edged sword.

The lessons I took away from all this eating drama in my family of origin were deep, wide, and hard to unlearn: Food is comfort. Food is love. Skinny is good. Fat is bad. In fact, nothing was worse or more disgusting in my mother's eyes than being fat. She rolled her eyes disgustedly at people who didn't fit into her very narrow view of acceptable. Even in her late years, she regularly disparaged our obese cat commenting, "Henri, you get fatter every day!" "Henri, you are as big as a house!" Perhaps she equates fat with lack of control: "How can people let themselves get so fat?" which made me wonder if it's actually the lack of control that she finds the most reprehensible.

Food became a losing battle for me. My internal dialogue went something like this: Eating people's food makes them like me. Not eating their food makes them dislike me. I want to eat; I want people to like me. Skinny is good, and fat is bad. Skinny is pretty, and fat is ugly. If I'm skinny and pretty, people feel threatened by me. If I'm fat and ugly, people don't feel threatened by me. I like to eat, and I like people to like me. Solution? Eat. Pretty twisted thinking, but I spent most of my life deeply entrenched in the religion of seeking approval.

When I was seventeen, I met a boy and fell in love. He fell in love with me too. And he also fell in love with my big ass, so for a long time, I didn't think too much about my weight. It's easier to feel good about yourself when you live with a person who constantly tells you how beautiful and sexy you are. Also, we were busy getting married and having kids. Well, we had a baby. Then we got married. Then we had two more.

Raising two daughters, I quickly realized I didn't want them to absorb all my body issues. Honestly, for many years I was too happy with my husband, my marriage, my babies, and my life to worry about being unhappy with my body and my weight anymore. No, I wasn't as skinny as my mother and sister, but I didn't care anymore. Plus, I lived in my own home and didn't have all the issues surrounding food shoved in my face every day.

Fast forward fifteen years when my elderly mother moved in with us following my dad's death. For the past several years, I'd embraced and loved my mom in a new way as she excelled in the grandma role. I let go of childhood hurts and found a beautiful new common ground with her in the mutual love of my children. However, when she moved in with us, the sweet relationship we'd cultivated over the past several years began to disintegrate. At this point in life, quitting smoking, having an unplanned mid-life baby, losing my dad, raising teenagers, preparing for my daughter to leave for college, and early menopause had taken their toll on my metabolism, and I weighed more than I ever had in my life.

Shortly after my mom moved in, I heard her through our shared wall gossiping to her friends and my siblings about me, my children, my housekeeping, my weight, my appearance, and so forth. Since I had recently quit smoking, I returned to my original source of comfort—food. Healthy food, junk food, sweet, salty, savory, it didn't matter, but I felt like I needed enough to fill me up and enough to make me big. Bigger than this tiny little woman who still seemed to wield some unseen power over me. Big enough to protect myself and my kids from her judgment, criticism, and meanness. And ultimately, big enough to cushion the bony little ragamuffin girl inside from her blows.

Mad as I was at her, I continued to eat the cookies she baked weekly so she wouldn't withdraw her love. Because saying no to the only olive branch of love she ever seemed to offer felt even worse than the gossip and criticism.

It is around this time that I met Geneen Roth. I didn't actually meet her, but when I read someone's writing—and after the first, I immediately devoured all her books—I often begin to feel like I know them intimately, like we're old friends, or at least like I can call her by her first name. Think about it; by this point you might feel like you know me pretty well, right? You actually do, whether you realize it or not. I've shared so much with you. Anyway, each of Geneen's books made me laugh, cry, feel understood, and they gave me tips.

I didn't shed a ridiculous amount of weight after reading Geneen's books. In fact, I may have even gained some. But at the same time, I gained peace of mind because my weight no longer affects me in the way it did for most of my life. While I still struggle sometimes, I think about my body and my weight in ways I never did before. I understand the issues in my life that brought me to this point, and I have lots of tools to help me climb out of the pit when I fall in.

That's the thing: You can't just deal with your weight. This is one of the many revelations I took away from Geneen's writing. She taught me how to deal with all of the things that caused me to overeat. I didn't need to exercise more; I needed to exercise more self-love. Was I a compulsive eater? Maybe. But I wasn't addicted to food. I was addicted to wanting to feel love, and the earliest expressions of love were delivered to me in the form of food. Was I a binge eater? Sometimes. But when the only sure form of comfort you can count on has always been a cream stick, then that's where you turn when you're sad. Taking away the source of comfort when you haven't dealt with issues is not self–care; in fact, it's cruelty.

Geneen's books brought the picture of what was going on in my life into sharper focus: the power I gave to food; the emotional energy stuffed into cookies, sandwiches, and chips; the fact that it was another part of my psyche that ate to protect that skinny little girl who cowered inside of me. I'm still working on changing things, and I probably always will be. I continue to address the issues that keep me feeling like I might need a little extra protection in the form of pounds, but I'm doing better. And that's all we're trying to do, right? Be a little better than we were yesterday?

One of my friends was painfully thin for most of her life. After her mother's death, she was finally able to feel peace, enjoy food, and reach a healthy and comfortable weight. There is a very dark part of me that wonders if I will release my extra weight when my mother passes away.

Today, I have a different picture of myself in my head. If I described myself to a police sketch artist now, the resulting portrait would likely be more beautiful than the person I see in the mirror, as the mirror reveals lines, wrinkles, and other imperfections that aren't in my mind's version of me. Now the image in my head is one reflected back from so many people who love me. The people who look at me and believe I'm already enough. Imagine how you look at your babies and remember that people look at you the same way. Some people think that the moon rises and sets in your eyes. Some people's whole worlds would be off kilter if your soul wasn't the sunrise in their universe every morning. Seeking these people, finding them, or awakening to realize they're already surrounding you is how you find your tribe and heal your soul.

My mother didn't teach me how to love my body or set a good example of a healthy self-image because she never knew how to do it herself. Yet, regardless of how it arrived or who the messenger was, my heart learned the lesson. Finding Geneen Roth's writing set me on the course to understand my issues with food and my weight. And because she shared her story, I was set free. It's our job to seek the teachers we need, and the Universe always provides them, if we open our eyes and hearts.

CHAPTER 3:
UNFUCK YOURSELF

"You know what the whores tell each other don't you? You take care of you."

> —Harry O. Swan, citing a conversation between Julia Roberts and Laura San Giacomo in Pretty Woman.

I HAVE SEEN A meme that says, "Unfuck Yourself. Be who you were before all that stuff happened that dimmed your fucking shine."

After becoming a mom, it seemed really clear to me that people should have some mandatory classes before they are given responsibility for a child. You need an education or at the very least some training to get a job— even the most basic minimum wage job. You have to take classes and practice to drive a car. But parenthood—the most important job anyone will ever have—well, just about anybody can do that. They offer a few courses in how to get the baby out of your body, but even those aren't necessary to be able to walk away from the hospital fully responsible for another human being.

We didn't take any classes. My parents didn't take any classes. Their parents didn't take any classes. They flew by the seats of their pants. They did what they knew and what they learned and never seemed to stop to ask, "Is this working?" I never knew my grandparents, but I've heard lots of stories, good and bad. I held a front row seat to the damage they inflicted on their own children and fell victim to their mistakes when my parents continued the cycle and inflicted more damage on us. I didn't want to continue that cycle any further and damage my kids, but in order to prevent future damage, you have to be aware of the past that caused it. Of course, in correcting your parents' mistakes, you'll often create a new set of mistakes with your own kids. At least I did.

My dad was the second of six children, and my mom was the second of four. Two middle children. I've always heard that oldest/youngest pairings generally work better than two oldest children, two youngest, or—God forbid—two middles. Of course, some people also think birth order is a lot of hogwash. I'd invite you to look at the relationship pairings around you—it's interesting.

My dad was born in 1916 to very poor parents. He grew up on a farm—owned by a wealthy family—where he and his family lived in return for his dad working the farm. My dad idolized his father; although, from most of the stories I've heard, he sounded like a nasty son of a bitch with a quick, violent temper who inflicted horrific beatings on his sons. One relative noted she was surprised my dad and his brothers even spoke to their father, much less idolized him, after how horribly he'd treated them.

I've heard very few stories about my grandfather, Harold. It always struck me as odd and narcissistic that he named two of his five sons, "Harry" (my dad) and "Harold" (my uncle).

The few oft repeated stories are:

Once, when my dad was about ten, he and his brother dropped the green top of a tomato onto his sister while she was using the outhouse. His sister was terrified of spiders and screamed bloody murder when she thought the tomato top was an arachnid. My dad jokingly recalls that he received the worst beating of his life.

When my parents started dating, my grandfather, upon learning my mother was Catholic, berated my father, "What the hell would you want with a goddamned redneck fish-eater?"

He called his eldest son's wife, "That white-haired bitch down in the gulley," and remarked that she was "so cheap she would chase a chicken down the road and back for a grain of corn."

After my dad read *The Magic of Believing*, by Claude Bristol, which proved life-changing for him, his father remarked, "He was a goddamned fool before he read that book, and he's an even bigger goddamned fool now." My mom often retold that story because she didn't subscribe to the magic of believing but fully supported my dad's being considered a fool.

Sounds like a real charmer, right? And these were the good stories.

My grandfather killed himself in his late sixties after being involved in a car accident, losing his license, and being faced with dependence on his wife for transportation. My dad found his dad's body. His only comment on his father's suicide was that even in death, the man had been efficient—shooting himself next to a drain in the basement so it wouldn't be a hardship for someone to clean up. I guess he didn't account for the emotional clean up. That's not quite as tidy. For the rest of his life, my dad blamed his mother for his dad's death. Although we never discussed it, it seemed to me, my grandfather must have carried around some very deep, unaddressed wounds. But men didn't exactly address their emotional health in the early 1900's. That wasn't very manly.

My dad spoke of his dad with reverence and respect. He even idolized John Wayne because he reminded him of his father. Although my dad had rage and anger issues, he was, at his core, loving and empathic. His own wounds ran deep, terrorized him, and manifested in rage and abuse, but he had a kind heart. Unfortunately, and I believe unwittingly, he created the same kind of hero worship in his own sons who never quite seemed to feel his acceptance of them until very late in life. Two of them never did.

Before meeting my mom, he led a wild life of partying, odd jobs, fame-seeking, minor league baseball, vocational agriculture teaching in Virginia where he started what has become one of the country's largest county fairs with some of his students, and opening a restaurant in northeast Ohio. It was this restaurant that my early twenty-something, English-teacher mom strolled into one day to grade papers—unintentionally stealing my dad's heart.

They tell different stories of their courtship. My dad's stories were wildly romantic and dripping with sentimentality. He said the first time he saw her, he didn't even see her face but watched her from behind as she walked across the parking lot to her car, and he said to his brother, "If I ever get married, I am gonna marry that girl." He said his brother responded that he was a fool, which seemed to be a common assumption. Years later, we'd found out that this was another "big fish" story. My dad, who was thirty-nine when he met my mom, had actually been married in his early twenties and divorced shortly before he married my mom, so, evidently, an "again" was missing from that little piece of Swan lore. Funny how one word can steal a story's magic.

Unfortunately, he died before I learned the truth, so I'll never know about his first marriage. Relatives told me our mom swore everyone in our family to silence and forbade them to speak of this first marriage. However, it sheds light on why my devout Catholic mom got married in a courtroom and not a cathedral. In the early days, she came back to the restaurant day after day, and he chatted with her week after week. He began inviting her out to fancy restaurants, taking her for drives in his shiny new Packard, and ultimately charming her into falling in love with him.

During their courtship, my mom and her friend went to Europe for six weeks. Although she never mentioned this, when cleaning out my parents' house after my dad's death, I found a scrapbook of this trip. Amidst the ticket stubs and pictures of landmarks and museums, I found miscellaneous pressed flowers and little cards addressed to: "Miss Cathy O'Loughlin, name of hotel, name of city."

"Mom, what are these?" I asked.

She rolled her eyes and said, "Oh, Dad sent me flowers everywhere I went."

I'm not sure at what point my parents began calling each other Mom and Dad, but I never remember them using each other's names other than occasionally when telling a story about the other. Once grandchildren began arriving, they referred to each other as Nanny and Papa. And often, my mom, as well as the rest of us, referred to my dad as Peach, a nickname one of my brothers coined for him, a play on the French word for father, "Pere."

Before Google and cell phones and social media, my dad found out where my mother would be staying at every stop on her trip and sent her flowers. I was equally blown away by the depth of my dad's romantic and thoughtful gestures and my mom's flippant dismissal of them.

My mom's stories of their courtship are far less romance-novel fodder. She mentioned more than once how she thought my dad was wealthy until she married him. Naturally, she was shocked when the shiny Packard he picked her up in was repossessed not long after they began sharing a home. And shortly after, a bill collector's visit informed her that the extravagant gifts and dinners that highlighted their courtship were bought on credit that was way over its limit.

Someone told me once that my brother Chris' rental house empire was about to come crashing down when he died and that could have been enough to prompt him to commit suicide. Again, we'll never know. He didn't leave a note or any indication that he'd checked out of his own accord. My parents rescued my brother from his debt posthumously. My dad couldn't stand the thought of his memory being tarnished by debt.

I inherited a lot of traits from my dad: Some unfavorable ones such as a quick temper and a vast vocabulary of profanity; some good ones such as empathy and childlike excitement. My mom and siblings and husband and kids rarely get as excited as I do—and sometimes wish they would—about little victories. I jump up and down, squeal, throw parties, and scream from rooftops. My girlfriend and I refer to these reactions as "parades and fireworks." In this way: "Hi. I did a thing. No one reacted in a significant way. Could you please lead the parade and fireworks? Thank you." I needed this especially after my dad's death. My dad's reaction to exciting news—even if that exciting news was, "I got these shoes for $20 at TJ Maxx!"—always exceeded my expectations. Share the tiniest bit of a happy update with him, and he'd laugh, whoop, throw his arms up in the air, hand you a $100 bill. He always delivered with parades and fireworks. That's the reaction I find myself anticipating sometimes. That's the reaction I have been missing since 2011.

I think he craved that reaction too because he loved to do things to make people happy. He would sometimes buy extravagant gifts such as a ridiculously expensive watch when I was sixteen, a pair of shoes he thought I should have because, "This is what they're wearing in New York." He gave me money with this specification, "Don't you dare do anything sensible with this." He liked to project an air of having plenty of money since he'd spent so much of his life without any, and finally, due in no small part to my mom's financial sensibility and frugality, he had a little bit squirreled away.

My dad retired when I was thirteen, so I spent a lot more one-on-one time with him than my siblings did. He had been a man who walked a few blocks through our neighborhood to his job in a local factory every morning. In the afternoon, my mom picked him up at the end of his shift. He came home for a home-cooked dinner, except on Fridays which was pizza or take-out fish dinners from a local pub. His evenings consisted of reading the paper, napping, watching the 6:00 local and 6:30 national news, followed by *Wheel of Fortune* and *Jeopardy!* He had strong opinions about what television shows we watched, and since for the better part of our childhood there was only one TV in the house, we watched what he wanted. Game shows. *Hee Haw. Lawrence Welk.* I remember the joy of half-day kindergarten, when I could watch three shows of my mother's choosing—*I Love Lucy, The Andy Griffith*

Show, and *Gomer Pyle, U.S.M.C.*—before my dad got home from work.

Usually, I rode along with my mom to pick him up from work in the afternoon. Before the days of seatbelt laws, I sat on the hump on the floor of the back seat so I could lean between them and listen to their conversations. Once, we got in a car accident on the way home. A car ran a stop sign and t-boned my mom's big Chevy Malibu. I ended up wedged between the soft burgundy velveteen upholstered driver and passenger seats, completely unharmed. My dad screamed, "MOM!" when the other car hit us. After the impact, she hissed, "Why are you screaming at me? What was I supposed to do?" He spent the rest of the day apologizing and explaining that it was just a gut reaction to scream out her name since she was driving.

When he retired at age seventy, his television-watching increased dramatically, and he experimented with new genres. He started watching soap operas, MTV—when it still played music videos—more game shows, though his favorites were always *The Price Is Right*, *Wheel of Fortune*, and *Jeopardy!*, *Magnum PI*, *Miami Vice*, and any sporting event he could find. In later years, he would even re-watch classic sports events, always with the sound off, which simultaneously entertained and annoyed my husband. One of his favorite new series was a Solid Gold or American Bandstand type of show called *Dance Party USA*. He watched it every day, and often I sat on the floor doing homework and watching with him. We discussed the various outfits— what was stylish and what seemed weird—who danced with whom—what seemed to be budding and ebbing relationships—and general dance skills. He always brought the same argument, "See that?" he'd say, pointing out a person moving around the floor, "That's how you are supposed to dance—with your feet, not your butt." Thank goodness he stopped watching before grinding became the popular form of dancing.

When he retired, our relationship shifted, and in many ways, he became more like a pal than my dad. We talked about everything. When my mom decided to send to me public school in eighth grade, after five years of homeschooling, I felt awkward and terrified. Since my mom didn't deal well with emotions, I talked with my dad about my fear. He encouraged and reassured me that I would be fine. He took me shopping and helped me pick out trendy clothes. The last thing I wanted was to draw attention to myself for having unfashionable clothes when starting at an inner-city junior high school.

Mostly, he attempted to boost my confidence by promising me I was just as pretty and smart and talented as the kids I would meet in junior high. In fact, since he was my dad, he assured me that I would be the prettiest, smartest, and most talented kid in the school. Although I recognized his bias and understood that most parents believe their kids are the cat's meow, it felt reassuring and deeply gratifying to believe that one person—my dad— truly thought of me as pretty, smart, and talented.

Throughout my teen years, I confided in my dad about issues in school and with peers; he listened and often offered pretty sound advice—considering he was in his seventies when I was in high school. We served as each other's liaison with my mother since she was often angry with one of us. When she was mad at me, he would tell me why and help me work it out. Conversely, sometimes he'd motion me into the family room and whisper, "Do you know why Nanny's pissed at me?" I would set out on a recon mission, sometimes uncovering the root of her anger, though usually powerless to affect any change in the situation.

The more time we spent together, the more I realized how alike we were and how much he loved seeing his reflection in me. We talked about everything. When I was sixteen, shortly after my brother Chris died, I suspected he was having an affair when a woman he golfed with periodically began calling the house. He kept a card from her on his bookshelf and her pictures also graced the stack of Polaroids beside his chair. I instantly disliked her. Despite the often strained and tumultuous relationship with my mom, I was fiercely loyal and protective of her and didn't want to see her played the fool.

One afternoon, I walked in the door and heard him on the phone. I lingered in the kitchen, knowing he didn't hear me, and eavesdropped on his conversation which ended with "I love you." This wasn't particularly uncommon since after my brother Chris died, my dad expressed his love with great freedom and abandon. Our family, many acquaintances, sometimes even telemarketers with whom he'd had a good chat got a heartfelt "I love you" before he hung up. This, however, felt different.

I stood in the doorway between the kitchen and the dining room, the same doorway of my earliest memory when he held me and I requested a coffee bottle, and asked him who he was talking to.

"Oh," he said, "just one of the guys I golf with."

I crossed my arms over my chest defiantly and countered, "Do you tell all your golfing buddies you love them?"

He slowly chuckled and hung his head sheepishly. "You know, darlin'," he said, pinning me with a stare that told me he knew I had him. "You aren't as smart as you think. There are lots of things you don't know and can't understand."

I said, "I understand more than you think."

What followed was a really uncomfortable conversation for any kid, even a grown one, to have with their parent, as my dad detailed the cold war that his marriage to my mom had become. I believed my dad was a passionate person who adored my mom and longed for her to return that love to him in his love language. I think he wanted to be cherished and revered. I'm not quite sure what my mom wanted or needed to feel cherished in their marriage, but I am pretty sure my dad fell short at providing it.

Now we had this heavy dark secret between us. He told my brother Brian also—we were the only children who remained living at home—so I had someone to process this with. What he told my brother about the situation sounded more like bragging about his relationship with a younger woman. A woman who, in fact, looked quite a bit like a younger version of my mom.

Once, he asked me to go golfing with her. He said he'd told her a great deal about me and that she would love to meet me. I asked him if he was out of his mind and suggested it would not be a good idea for us to be in such close proximity with a bag of potential weapons at the ready.

For the next few years, our relationship continued in this sometimes-awkward friendship. He told me way too much information about his personal life. I told him enough about mine to make him happy and feel as if he was in the loop. He offered a unique perspective on a lot of my high school problems, especially since he had become more tolerant and calmer in his seventies. He didn't yell as much, and after one final incident, he never hit me.

I remember very clearly the last two times he hit me. One, I was on the phone, and he wanted me to carry something upstairs. Evidently, I didn't move quickly enough, and I don't remember clearly if he yelled first and I yelled back, but I very clearly remember him grabbing the receiver from my hand and hitting me across the face with it. Later, he apologized. Later still, I forgave him. But I never let him forget it.

In his favorite movie, *Pretty Woman*, fittingly enough, there's a scene when George from *Seinfeld* (Jason Alexander) hits Julia Roberts across the face and she says, "How do men know how to hit you in the spot right above your cheekbone and it feels like your eye is going to explode?" For years after, every time we watched the movie and that part came on, I would say, "Just like the time you hit me with the phone." He sighed and sometimes silent tears would fall down his cheeks. At the time I felt some gratification knowing that he regretted hurting me, and years later, I felt deep regret and sadness for reminding him of the times he fell short and gave into his rage.

The last time he hit me, I was eighteen. I had gone out and came home to change before heading to another party. I had been drinking, but I wasn't driving. Someone else, who may or may not have been drinking, was picking me up. My dad didn't know that and was trying to prevent me from leaving. Yelling, screaming, and shoving ensued. I was much smaller than my dad but a worthy adversary because I was so angry; imagine a wet cat. He had me pinned against the wall when my brother Rich came in and pulled him off me. Calmly, he told my dad, "Let her go. She's not driving." And he did.

My mom sat less than five feet away at the kitchen table calmly reading a book. True to form, she had ignored this whole scene and not said a word or lifted a finger to help me. I was so mad that I wanted to pick up her whole chair and dump her out on the floor. Instead, I flipped her book into her lap, and when she looked up at me stunned, I said, "Fuck you for never sticking up for me." As far as I know, that was the last time anyone got beat. Of course, by this time, I was eighteen, and all my brothers except Brian had moved out. Additionally, my dad was significantly mellower in his old age.

Our relationship continued to improve. There were slip-ups here and there, and I got angry at him from time to time, but for the next twenty years, the main feeling I felt for my dad was adoration. I was especially grateful that as he aged, layers of bad fell away, allowing the goodness to shine through more clearly.

Some people get older and cranky, but my dad seemed to get happier and kinder as he aged. The last time I visited him, I was worried about him. His color wasn't good, and his eyes appeared sunken in. Although he was in his favorite chair, he didn't light up the way he usually did when I walked in. I thought that he was sad or sick, and I sat down on his lap and put my hand on his cheek. "What's the matter, Papa?"

He chuckled as he patted my hand and said, "Nothing's the matter, darlin'. I'm just old and tired."

It took me a long time to see what I see now, as is usually the case, in hindsight. My dad gave me a foundation of love. He had a lot of flaws, including the fact that he was physically and verbally abusive. However, he also told me I was beautiful, smart, and could do whatever I put my mind to. Usually, we hear the bad and ignore the good though, so my mom's criticisms often overshadowed his cheers.

Now, I am grateful for the clarity time and perspective have afforded me. My husband is very different from my dad. Quiet, calm, and even-tempered, he loves me fiercely just like my dad did. Sometimes, we can't see the good people are bringing us because it's buried by behavior that's rooted in their own wounds. When we are able to strip away the behavior that's not about us, we can often unveil the love that is.

CHAPTER 4:
YOU SHOULD BE
ASHAMED OF YOURSELF

"If we can share our story with someone who responds with empathy and understanding, shame can't survive."
—*Dr. Brené Brown*

"YOU SHOULD BE ASHAMED of yourself." Shame was a go-to parenting intervention in many families in the 1970s, my family of origin included. Sometimes it was lazily doled out to correct some inappropriate childish behavior such as not cleaning your dinner plate when your mother slaved to make a delicious meal, and children were starving in Africa. Truth be told, I was always more than willing to give my meatloaf to any starving children, but the one time I offered, I was smacked and sent to my room for being a smart aleck. As a child, I had no problem stopping eating when I was full, but I was often coerced into eating more.

Other times, that shame arrow stuck directly into the deepest part of my soul, wreaking havoc on my psyche. Those times, it wasn't about food.

When Brad and I began the parenting journey and had to decide on how to discipline our own children, I immediately outlawed, "You should be ashamed of yourself," and "What's the matter with you?" Those oft-repeated phrases still rattled around in my brain all too frequently, and I didn't think anyone, especially our children, needed assistance to feel shame.

However, until I read all of Dr. Brené Brown's books, my idea of shame's destructiveness barely scraped the surface. Brené (we're on a first name basis, obviously, since she's seen the depths of my soul) puts it into perspective by differentiating guilt and shame like this: Guilt—I did something bad. Shame—I *am* bad. I had dealt with guilt, even getting it to a manageable level. But shame... goodness, I hadn't even opened that door.

I've mentioned that my family of origin was all about appearances. It didn't matter what was actually going on, as long as everything looked okay from the outside. It didn't matter how you felt, as long as you smiled and used good manners. My parents really didn't seem to care much about what *actually went on,* as long as things looked okay on the surface. My mom never appeared to be in touch with her feelings; therefore, feelings weren't important. She seemed to believe that her way of cooking, eating, dressing, believing, loving, and being was right. Anyone who disagreed was a moron. That being said, the truth didn't matter; the façade did. Smile, pretend nothing happened, and don't you dare talk about it.

Naturally, when I write about what actually happened in my family, people get uncomfortable—especially the people in my family. Most especially the ones who are still going along with my mom's practice of pretending nothing happened. While I do my best to share only my experiences without drawing anyone in, sometimes they intersect.

A few months ago, my mom pointed out a relative's unfortunate childhood saying, "I don't think she had too many happy holidays growing up." I asked my mom if she had ever been present for any holidays in our house. When we were younger, most acts of disobedience or perceived disrespect resulted in a beating. Not a spanking—a beating. Once, when I was ten, my dad beat me with a red plastic baseball bat because my toddler nephew fell down. It was my fault that he was running, evidently. It didn't even have to be disobedience or disrespect; it could be that my dad perceived someone was being lazy, stupid, or millions of other derogatory adjectives that wound him up. It could be that my dad was just in a bad mood or irritated about something.

As we got older, a fight or rude comment often resulted in someone storming out. One sibling or another refused to attend holidays because they disliked other siblings who would be in attendance. My dad usually had at least one screaming fit. The day often ended with everyone retreating to their separate corners, silently seething. I didn't have very many happy holidays growing up either. Once, my mom recounts, my dad took my brothers to the basement for some infraction and beat them with a board—his paddle of choice was a 2 x 4—on Mother's Day. She threatened to divorce him because, as she recalled, "You've ruined every holiday for me, and now you ruined Mother's Day too." When she told me this, my stomach flopped, because implicit in her statement was this: She was upset that he ruined her day not that he beat their children.

For my entire life—until our childhood home was sold—every time I walked into that house for any sort of celebration, my stomach immediately twisted into knots. Others, who saw only the outside of that sky-blue and cream, glass house, remember our family as happy and loving. People felt so bad when my brothers died. How could such terrible things happen to such a wonderful family? Things are rarely as wonderful as they seem on the outside.

A few years ago, I published a blog in which I told some unpleasant truths about the abuse that had occurred in my family throughout my childhood. A dear friend who had provided a lifeline for me during one of the worst times in my life, after my brother Chris died, called and lit into me. She was appalled by what I'd written and accused, "You were spoiled rotten, the apple of your dad's eye. How can you say this horrible stuff about your family?" The horrible stuff was the truth. Being the apple of my dad's eye was a paradox. I loved him. I hated him. I wanted to please him and to defy him. I wanted his acceptance, but I learned the hard way that seeking his acceptance often ended tragically.

For a long time, I wondered how some of my siblings and I survived while our two brothers didn't. Part of me wonders if my survival was wrapped up in my ability to take flight. Emotionally and physically. From the time I was very little, I left my body. I learned from a psychiatrist friend, this phenomenon is called dissociation. At the time, it was just a weird feeling of looking down from above at a sad little ragamuffin girl who wasn't me. The me who was outside my body looking at that sad little girl felt strong, invincible, and untouchable. Unfortunately, or perhaps fortunately, I was never able to harness this power. Now, I wish that I had tried a little harder. It was a pleasant escape, and it would have been magical to willfully project myself out of my own little body and reality.

A good part of the time I was in my body was spent figuring out how to protect various members: excusing my dad's temper and my mom's emotional unavailability, explaining away or avoiding the truth of my brothers' drug addictions and later suicide, rationalizing what I perceived as my sister's dislike of me, justifying my brothers' false bravado, minimizing, and normalizing. Trying to make the inside look like the outside.

For too long, I believed that if I loved people enough, everything would be okay. If I could be good enough, smart enough, kind enough, pretty enough, skinny enough... Maybe if I could be invisible. Maybe if I could be more visible. Maybe if I could drink enough vodka or smoke enough cigarettes or sleep with enough boys, they would look at me and really see me. I couldn't do enough or be enough or love enough or sacrifice enough or mess up enough because nothing that was wrong with the people in my family was ever within my control.

My dad's issues were his own—his abusive father and anger toward his mother. My mom obviously had issues too, but she was closed off and didn't talk about them. She wore stoicism and sarcasm as her protective armor. She prided herself on never showing any emotion or lack of control, which she seemed to view as weakness. My family's issues and my issues were about us. They were about my sister and my mom and my dad and my brothers. They were about the wounds they inflicted on each other and those that were inflicted by the people who had harmed them so irreparably. None of them were ever about me. How could I fix what so many others had broken into so many pieces? I couldn't. But I also couldn't stop their broken pieces from cutting me, jabbing me, and getting stuck in my yet-to-be-toughened-up-thin-skinned flesh.

It was a dual assault. In my mind, the outside wasn't good enough, and since no one seemed to care what was on the inside, that must be pretty pathetic as well.

While I sometimes make people uncomfortable now by telling the truth, as a child, I fabricated outrageous stories. Since I lived only part-time in that body, it was relatively easy to make up an idealized life rather than to tell the truth. We weren't encouraged to tell the whole truth anyway. Who wanted to hear the truth that my dad abused us while my mom looked the other way? Or the truth that my brothers did drugs and abused each other and me. Fuck that. Why not invent a better story?

My mom gave us multi-syllable names since our last name was short, one syllable. But Elizabeth, Jonathan, Christopher, David, Brian, Richard, and Mary Catherine became Beth, Jon, Chris, Dave, Bri, Rich and Poo. Beth, the first child, is fifteen years older than I am. After her came our five brothers, and then me. My earliest memories of my sister involve her telling me to get out of her room. Get away from her. Stop touching her. Stop begging to play with her long hair. My god-sister came to visit one time and let me play with her long hair—it was the 70's and all the cool girls had long straight hair. Mine was short and wavy. In my memory, my sister seemed irritated at best and disgusted at worst with my existence. She appeared annoyed by the fact that she had to share a home—or even a planet—with me. Years later, when I had two daughters who were thirteen years apart, I realized how difficult it is to be a teenager with a much younger sister.

My sister had a certain perfume, which like everything else about her, was off limits to me. Sometimes, I sneaked into her room while she was gone and smelled it. To this day, although our relationship has had many ups and downs and we've had varying degrees of closeness and distance, this perfume is always the scent connected to her in my mind.

As a little girl, when it felt like she didn't want a relationship with me, I sought out sister relationships with other girls I encountered. For most of my life, I have been cultivating a mom or a sister relationship with nearly every woman I met. *Side note: That panned out, since today, I'm surrounded today by lots of amazing women who are my soul sisters.* The relationship between my sister and mother was also fraught with conflict, and sometimes, I got thrust into the middle. In hindsight, I wonder if my mom subconsciously sought to correct perceived mistakes she made with my sister in parenting me. I wonder if she tried to foster a closer relationship with me since she and my sister didn't seem to have much of a bond. My mom rarely delved into introspection, so it's not a conversation we ever had.

Still, through a lack of self-awareness, perhaps sprinkled with a pinch of unchecked narcissism, she created a hostile triangulated relationship among the three of us which continued for at least forty years. When I was nine, my sister gave birth to her first child, and I was overjoyed to be an aunt to this precious boy. I loved babies, so having access to this little cherub who loved me felt like the most magical thing that had ever happened. In rapid succession, she had three more babies, and I was thrilled for the new roles of aunt and babysitter.

These new roles also afforded me alone time with my sister—a new occurrence. She proved to be a loyal confidante, a wealth of advice, and a good sounding board for complaints about our mother when I was a teenager.

She also told me some things about our mother from her own adolescent and teenage experience of her. And sometimes, she told me how spoiled I was.

Once, during a low point in my relationship with my sister, my closest—in age—brother told me, "She hates you. She's always hated you. She's always going to hate you. Stop trying to make her like you. All you're doing is making yourself look pathetic." No one can cut to the quick of family dynamics like a sibling.

The cards were not stacked in our favor from the start. In my opinion, my sister is very much like my mother, although I don't think either of them would agree with that assessment. Regardless, their similarities flowed like a steady stream of gasoline on the lit fuse of a competitive and volatile relationship.

When my sister married a man that my parents didn't initially approve of, and I married a man they liked, the divide between us got deeper and wider.

Finally, compounding my sister's perception of me as spoiled, my dad blatantly treated my children differently than hers. More than once, she referred to my kids as spoiled brats, based mostly on the way my parents treated them. I truly believe my mother tried to treat all of her grandchildren fairly, but just like he did with his own kids, my dad played favorites.

Despite the strains on our relationship, I loved and looked up to my sister. Several times, when I needed her, she showed up for me. She took me to Planned Parenthood and acted as my guardian when I was fifteen so I could get birth control. She was the first person I called when I quit the birth control and found myself pregnant at twenty, and she comforted and encouraged me. When I found myself expecting another unplanned baby at thirty-three, she threw me a baby shower. At times, I wondered if her actions came from love and concern for me or if helping me gave her the gratification of being needed as well as a feeling of superiority, but her motivation doesn't change my gratitude for the times she showed up. A few times, I even thought we would have the sister relationship I craved; unfortunately, lofty expectations can quickly turn to resentments. Ultimately, I have accepted our relationship for what it is after years of craving more.

Since my actual sister relationship was never the one I wanted, I sought out idealized sister relationships with the girls my brothers dated. A few of them actually did a great job of filling the perfect big sister role. Especially Chris' girlfriends. Chris used to take me lots of places with him, and he often told girls he dated that if I didn't like them, they were out. One of his first serious girlfriends took me horseback riding and bought me fun little girly gifts like purses, lip gloss, and perfume.

His next serious girlfriend really became the sister I'd dreamed of. We shared secrets, shopped together, hung out, and watched movies. She was my most loyal confidante and became one of my first real girlfriends. After Chris' death, she remained one of my best friends. I would call her late at night when she was away at college, and she talked me through puberty, periods, girl drama, boyfriend trouble, first loves, and so much more. She would tell me exciting stories about her college experiences. Our relationship was the sister relationship I'd always wanted.

She let me drive her cute little sports car, and when she and Chris broke up, I was the angriest I'd ever been at him. We stayed close after their relationship ended, and she never made me feel uncomfortable for loving him still or guilty for having a relationship with his new girlfriend. She was kind, sweet, and in my eyes, the perfect sister. When my oldest brother, Jon, got married—the year after Chris' death—we were both bridesmaids in his wedding and rode to New York with my parents and siblings in a rented conversion van, laughing and playing games. A few years later, she tragically died of cancer at twenty-six, leaving me with a broken heart, a renewed sense of loneliness, and the jewelry my brother had given her as gifts during their relationship.

Despite the love, faith, and trust I felt for her, I couldn't share one issue, the deepest source of my shame that gnawed at me for forty years of my life. The memory of this experience, when I engaged with it, rendered me incapable of reconciling what happened into who I am. It prohibited me from being a full and complete person.

When I was very young, my closest brother and I slept in the same bedroom for a period of time. During this time, we engaged in different sexual acts, him touching me and my touching him. At the time, I was probably four or five, and he was seven or eight. While this felt debilitating to me, when I struck up a few conversations—hypothetically of course—with people about this type of behavior, they said some version of, "It's pretty normal for kids to experiment."

I love my brother, thought of him as my best friend for most of my life, and wanted his attention. I remember feeling we shouldn't do these things, but I couldn't completely process it, and it happened before I was old enough to confess anything to the man on the other side of the screen who could absolve me from the stain it left on my soul. Perhaps that is why the stain remained for so long.

One time, one of my parents walked in when we were playing some version of this "game." I don't remember what they said or did. My brother told me later that my dad told him, "Don't do that with your little sister." Our family didn't talk about sex. Our genitalia were referred to as "puddle-makers" as in: Your genitals were for urinating. Period. Imagine how bizarre it was years later when my aging dad became overly sexualized and told my newly married twenty-two-year-old self that he hoped I gave my husband a blow job once in awhile because that's what men went to hookers for. More *Pretty Woman* wisdom, I imagine.

But when we were children, neither of my parents spoke to us about what was happening. They just moved us to separate rooms. Rich and I didn't speak of it for years, and I never told anyone. When I was a teenager, I made up a story about being molested by an uncle. I'm not sure what motivated me to tell this lie. Perhaps I was gauging people's reaction, dipping my toe in the water to see if they would walk away if they knew this shameful part of my past.

About twenty years later, after our older brother, Brian, had committed suicide, I sought therapy. One night, Rich called me very late, very drunk. He said, "Do you remember what happened when we were little?" I told him I did, and I thought it was something normal little kids did. I didn't really believe that at the time, but I wanted to. He said, "Normal kids don't do that."

I still never told anyone.

Close to twenty more years passed, and my brother sent me a segment of a creative fiction "memoir" he'd been working on. Many parts were funny and enjoyable, and Brad and I sat side-by-side laughing and often crying at the exaggerated exploits of my kind-of-fictional family. In one section, my brother described similar events as to what happened in our childhood, embellished of course in his characteristic way. My husband and I read this simultaneously. I tried to close the document, but it was too late. He simply asked, "Is this true?"

I cried for days. I was mortified, ashamed, and certain that my perfect husband would leave me. Surely, after all the nonsense he'd witnessed and been subjected to since marrying into the Swan family, this would be the final act that would push him over the edge. This would be too much.

But he wasn't mad at me. He didn't leave. In fact, he said, "Honey, you were a little girl. You guys were kids. It wasn't your fault. What if that had happened to our girls? You certainly wouldn't have blamed them. No one would. Your family was fucked up, and you should never have had to carry this around with you all these years."

Like Brené says, "If we can share our story with someone who responds with empathy and understanding, shame can't survive."

While that was the beginning of my healing, climbing out from under that intense cloak of shame was a struggle. It took a long time to silence the recording in my head that claimed: You are bad and unworthy of love and acceptance.

"You're not a bad person. You're a very good person who bad things have happened to... We've all got both light and dark inside us. What matters is the part we choose to act on. That's who we really are." – Sirius Black in *Harry Potter and The Order of the Phoenix* by J.K. Rowling.

Brown describes shame as lethal, saying that it needs secrecy, silence, and judgment to grow. These, of course, are the things we are most willing to feed it.

I struggled for years trying to process what happened. Did it happen to me? Was I complicit? Was it even such a big deal? I never blamed my brother; we were little kids. And yet, for years, I carried residual shame, guilt, and resentment that impaired my relationships with my family of origin. I was so angry at them for perpetuating the big lie that our childhood was a good and fun-filled time.

I have devoured every book Brené Brown wrote. Listening repeatedly to her TED Talks and rumbling with my own past has brought me to a place where I have finally spoken about this to a few trusted people. And look: Now, I've just told all of you.

Reading Brown's books showed me that healing was as close as bringing the dark secrets into the light. It's true: Shame cannot survive being spoken of and met with empathy. Shame tells us that we are bad people. We're outcasts. We're the others. Shame tells us that we are unlovable, unworthy, flawed, fucked-up, and as long as we let that voice keep us quiet, we will remain imprisoned in our shame. We can't get past the pain until we actually go through the pain. You know the old refrain: You can't go over it, can't go under it, can't go around it, you have to go through it. But when you do, finally, you can move on.

Sharing the events that keep us locked in a prison of shame is extremely difficult, and I don't recommend that you randomly tell your life story to a friendly person on a train. I don't recommend telling it to just anyone. In fact, sharing your shame story in the wrong forum or with the wrong person could be even more damaging. Have you ever shared with someone and then had them criticize or minimize or one-up your story? It feels shitty, and it can make you condemn yourself and second guess sharing again. You aren't wrong; you just shared with the wrong person, and unfortunately, for whatever reasons—most likely their own baggage and bullshit—the person wasn't able to be with you, empathize, hold space for your story, and that feels horrible. Don't let a bad experience pull you back into the shame vortex. You will find people who will be more than willing to listen, empathize, hold space for your stories and your experiences. You will find people who offer compassion and unconditional positive regard. Maybe it will be a therapist, a friend, someone you meet at church or in a book club or in a support group who shares similar interests. Perhaps it's not an actual person but a character in a book or movie that overcomes a hardship and gives you a sense of hope. Sometimes, writing a painful story down in a letter, even one that will never be sent or read by anyone else, can be a great step toward healing. Be advised, some people might walk away if you show them a dark part of you. Some people won't be able to hear your truth because it will trigger a shame reaction in them that they can't or won't process. Please hear me: These are not your people. This is not your tribe. They have their own shit to deal with. Your people? Your people will listen. They'll stay. They'll meet you where you are, stay with you, and love you right through the pain.

When I shared my darkest, most horrific secret with my husband, he didn't get mad at me. He didn't think I was a bad person. His feelings about me didn't change at all. He wrapped me up in his arms and told me he loved me. He said that he was sorry for what I had been through and sorrier that I'd carried the shame of it around with me for forty years. He told me that I wasn't bad or broken or fucked up. In just a few minutes, he refuted all the lies that shame had been telling me for four decades. He freed me from the secret I'd carried around for so long, festering and poisoning my soul. And that was it. Nearly forty years of shame vanished. It didn't happen overnight, but it happened. Shame cannot survive being spoken about and met with empathy. Believe it.

This story has kept me from publishing this book for almost five years. I never wanted sharing it to feel vengeful, and I never wanted to hurt my brother who is truly my friend. I've written and rewritten it in many different ways, but I have come to this realization: It will never feel comfortable, but it finally feels complete. Last week, I shared the story with my therapist. She said, "Did you ever think that maybe this was just a way for two little kids to try to feel safe in a house that didn't feel safe?" I hadn't. But I do now.

CHAPTER 5:
A SEMI-CHARMED LIFE

"Love is not warm and fuzzy or sweet and sticky. Real love is tough as nails. It's having your heart ripped out, putting it back together, and the next day, offering it back to the same world that just tore it up."

—*Glennon Doyle*

YOU NEVER HAVE ANY idea what a person's life is like unless they tell you. Really. Their nitty gritty inside details and what makes them tick. You can look at a friend's beautifully filtered Instagram pictures and think, "Wow, her life is so perfect. Her kids are always dressed so nicely and smiling." You may see this and not realize that she is posting those pictures to try to cheer herself out of a life mired in the soul-crushing swamp of depression.

A few years ago, we belonged to a church, and I was part of the "impact" committee. That was progressive Christianese for the people who greet guests, make them feel welcome, invite them to enjoy a cup of coffee or see if they need to know where anything is. Week after week, I'd smile and hug and shake hands with a few hundred people, but once, a woman stopped me and said, "How do you always have it so together?"

"I beg your pardon?" I laughed.

"You do," she continued. "You're always dressed nicely and smiling, and your little family is so cute."

She didn't see me try on outfit after outfit that morning, trying to find one that hid the extra twenty pounds I carried shamefully. She didn't know that my cute little family spent the morning fighting or that I had screamed and sworn at them to hurry up so we weren't late to church. She didn't realize that my husband was nursing a grudge in the corner because he didn't want to be at church, and she surely had no way of knowing that my adorable daughter and son had argued the entire way. You just don't know. You can't judge what's on the inside by how pretty the package is.

A few years ago, someone told me that she was jealous of my fairy-tale perfect life and that Brad and I were "meant to be." I thought a lot about that for a long time. For a while, I would have agreed that at the very least, we were brought together in a divine appointment. Then, "meant to be" started to feel patronizing. I didn't like that people wrote off our happy marriage as, "Oh, they were meant to be." As if our marriage was the result of luck or a gift, or that it was easy or untouchable. At any given point along the way, we could have decided not to be anymore, and then what? If some divine or universal force intended our souls to become one and we took a different route, would it cause some cataclysmic uproar? If we were destined to be together by some higher power who knew far better than we what our souls needed, then loving each other should be easy. Staying together should be a piece of cake.

But it's not.

In fact, in the twenty-nine years we've been together, the sad moments have been just as plentiful as the happy ones. For as many times as we felt blissful and in love, we experienced dark moments where we wanted to shank the other. You read that right. Shank.

Sometimes, when I find a comment condescending or patronizing, I respond by saying shocking things. A verbal touché, if you will.

Once, early in our marriage when my mother-in-law offered some helpful comments on how to improve a meal I made, I countered with, "He married me for the blow jobs, not the meatloaf." My mother-in-law took it in stride however laughing, "I just never know what will come out of your mouth."

When I met my husband in the back of our friend's Cutlass on a rainy evening in 1990, I didn't know we were meant to be. When we hooked up later that evening and on subsequent evenings, it wasn't abundantly clear that this boy with braces, a Triple Fat Goose coat and a backward baseball cap was my destiny. In fact, through most of our marriage, it hasn't been crystal clear that we were meant to be.

When the universe united us, it didn't specify that we would go through seven levels of hell together. That some days, we would feel less love and more disdain for each other. That over the course of our charmed life together, we'd bury my brother and my dad, lose money, patience, hope, and faith. It never indicated that we'd make and lose friendships. There was no promise that we wouldn't fall out of love one day and wonder if it had all been a series of unfortunate choices. You would think people who were meant to be would have it easier than all that. And that was just the first twenty years. We got married young. We could easily have forty or fifty more years in us.

On most days, I wake up happy to be married to a man I admire and respect and cherish. And on some days, I wake up and think: Who leaves for work and doesn't take out the garbage? A selfish garbage person, that's who.

When I met this sometimes-wonderful-sometimes-garbage-person, I felt like a shattered human. I had lost my brother, Chris, and with him, I lost my faith. Chris used to reassure my worried and nervous self by promising me, "You don't have to worry about anything happening to anyone as long as I'm around. I'll always save us." He'd promised. But then he was gone. The person I'd counted on to save all of us couldn't save himself, and life began to feel precarious and unsafe.

Brad, however, felt safe. We were not particularly interested in each other at first, so there seemed to be a relatively low potential for heartbreak. Evidently, meeting your soul mate or destiny doesn't seem like much of anything, at least it didn't for either of us. Lust, sure, but we were teenagers with raging hormones. Still, this shy, quiet boy with the blackest eyes I've ever seen, wormed his way into my heart before I even realized that I needed to put up my walls. He was only about my size and had the most beautiful lips I'd ever seen. Also, he called me "dear." Dear. It was maybe the cutest thing I had ever heard. He was sixteen.

The first time I kissed his beautiful lips, I thought I could probably be happy kissing them for the rest of my life and told my friend that. She told me to go to bed because I was drunk. I was. But I do still get goosebumps kissing those lips.

We spent the next three years drinking excessively, smoking excessively, fighting excessively, and falling recklessly, wildly, and hopelessly in love. We broke up several times a month, partly for the thrill of getting back together. By the time we got to college, the drinking, partying, jealousy, and fighting had gotten to be too much, and we took a break. Except, a few days into that break, I found out that I was pregnant.

We reacted and fought and accused and cried and argued, and I decided to go live with my brother in New York. Actually, I didn't tell anyone this plan until later. In fact, I just tagged along on a road trip with my dad to move Rich to New Jersey and then to visit Jon in New York. Secretly, I planned to stay in New York.

When we got to Jon's, I wanted to go to the city— Greenwich Village specifically. In my immature and hormone-fueled dreams, my baby and I would live in a cute little studio apartment where I would write and we would have a magnificent metropolitan life. As we strolled through the city in the August heat, I informed my dad of my plan. He listened, not saying much. When I finished, he simply said, "You know, staying here... keeping the baby away... you would break that boy's heart."

Until then, I hadn't really thought about anyone or anything but myself and the tiny life growing inside me. I wanted to get away from everything that could hurt us. I wanted to protect her from the pain that had permeated my childhood. I didn't stop to think that I had already ensured us a better life by falling in love with the best man I have ever known who would be her dad.

I have been burned a time or two or twenty by loving who-I-believed-someone-could-become instead of who they actually were. My dad used to tell me, "If you think you can change someone, run the other way." I've been shocked and hurt by people over and over. While I didn't fall in love with Brad with the idea that I wanted to or could change him, as life progressed, I did wish he would change.

More than once, in conversations about relationships, people, mostly women, have questioned, "Did you marry your dad?" Lots of people do, I guess, and I have always hoped that my girls will one day "marry their dad." I did not, though. As much as I adored my dad, I married someone almost completely opposite of him. Brad rarely gets mad, hardly ever yells, and never raises a hand in anger to anyone. He is as even and calm as my dad was unpredictable. So, no, I didn't marry my dad. The funny thing is, after I married him, I tried to change him to make him more like my dad. I got mad at him for being indifferent, for not being passionate enough, for not getting excited all the time. It took me nearly twenty years to realize that my dad's romanticism and charm was the light side of the same passion that spurred angry beatings in its darker manifestation—the dark side was what I was running from when I ran smack into Brad.

Sometimes, I thought he was a lifeline God threw me when I was drowning. He is calm and rational and patient. He didn't cheat or flirt or overpower or talk down or try to manipulate. He never wanted to stop me from being me. Although, we did fight about that for a while when I went through a phase of thinking that the real me was someone who wanted to flirt and dance with and kiss other men besides my husband. That person was only unleashed when I'd had more than a few drinks.

I think that's a common misconception—that alcohol or drugs somehow enable us to be who we really are. I would wake up after those nights feeling so guilty and ashamed of what I'd done, what I'd said, how I'd acted. I was obviously too caught up in this identity crisis to question the irony, but now, I see quite clearly: Being who you really are never makes you feel shame.

After several years and lots of fights, I realized that the drunk me wasn't the real me. It was just some facet of my personality. Like we all have light and dark. There is some dark murky shit in me, and it poured out when I drank too much vodka. Or rum, or beer.

When I was finally able to step back and analyze the situation, it made zero sense that we would need a chemical intervention except those prescribed by a professional to be our best selves. Yes, we should go into the dark of our psyche and explore our demons. We don't, however, need to bring them out and set them at the table for dinner. And we certainly should not mistake our shadow self for our true self.

The person I was when I drank too much could be a quite a lot of fun. She was flirtatious and silly and giddy. She had no boundaries, though, and often crossed lines and unintentionally hurt people's feelings. Brad liked her very much when she contained her flirting to him. It took me a little too long to figure out that it was not that my husband liked me better when I was drunk, but that he likes me to flirt with him. I don't even need a drop of alcohol for that.

It took me nearly thirty years and three children to fully trust him and believe that he would never leave me. Do I think we're meant to be? No. I believe we decided to be. Over and over, each time we were faced with the choice, we ultimately chose each other. We continue to face happiness and hardship, accomplishments and adversity, tears and triumphs. That's just life.

Still, far too often, I lose sight of everything that he does right and get caught up in an empty gas tank or a forgotten garbage can. Sometimes I lose sight of who he is: A man who day after day, year after year, collects me piece by piece and shard after jagged shard—sharp edges and soft curves—and wraps each part in love until I am myself—full and whole. I can't even guess what fresh hell and wonderful delights await us in the years to come of our fairy-tale life. I know that whatever it is, I'll be able to handle it better with my hand in his.

CHAPTER 6:
WHAT ARE YOU
SO AFRAID OF?

"Our deepest fear is not that we are inadequate. Our deepest fear is that we are powerful beyond measure. It is our Light, not our Darkness, that most frightens us."
—Marianne Williamson

WHEN I WAS THIRTY, I quit a job that I loved for a job that paid more money. It seemed like an appropriate choice for a person in her thirties. At least earning money seemed like what I was supposed to be doing in my thirties. Instead of pursuing success through happiness, I pursued happiness through success. I don't really give a lot of energy to regrets, but I have often felt regret about leaving that job. It was a cool environment, filled with creative, smart, passionate people, and more than once, I've looked back fondly on my time there and wondered "what if?"

However, I know now that if I hadn't left that job, I never would have walked through the door that led me to one of my greatest teachers and friends.

The job that I took for the money felt a lot like white collar prostitution. I mean, it didn't require actual sexual favors, but in selling printing services, more often than not, I was also selling myself. The printing jobs I sold during my short time at this job were probably based more on people liking, trusting, and maybe wanting to spend more time with me and less on the quality of the printing. Once, I got a very small two-color job from a guy who then wanted to come in for a tour and press okay. This was a huge printing company that specialized in full-color catalogs, brochures, and more. Perhaps this is just sales or printing in general. At least, that was my jaded perspective of it in the early 2000s.

When I took the job, my boss promised me that once I completed my training, I could work from home like the other salespeople did. That never happened. In fact, a few months down the road, when I inquired about when I could start working from home, he winked and answered, "It's good for morale to have you here."

Wanting to be certain that he meant what I thought he meant, I responded frankly, "You mean the guys in the plant like to look at me?"

He said, "We all like to look at you."

He wasn't lying. Once, in a sales meeting, shortly after camera phones made their way into the hands of nearly every cell phone owner, the production manager interrupted a meeting to ask my boss if he was going to pay attention to the information he was going over or if he was just going to take pictures of me on his new phone. At the time though, letting men ogling me seemed a worthy tradeoff for a good salary, great benefits, a car allowance, gas and corporate credit cards, and a lot of freedom.

It was a weird, sometimes creepy environment, but despite my almost pathological penchant for being suspicious and apprehensive of men, I never felt threatened by any of the men who worked there. No one ever touched me or attempted to, In fact, most of the men were kind and respectful. The instances of inappropriate behavior were confined to loosely veiled innuendo. One manager—who repeatedly reminded my often-inappropriate boss to "watch the video," referencing a training video on sexual harassment in the workplace—was an honest family man with integrity who became my friend and ally. I trusted and respected him and believed he would have come to my aid if I ever needed protection, though it never came to that.

All of this nonsense aside, I was incredibly inspired by the women there. They were these amazingly strong and independent, badass women who basically ran the joint and took no shit from the men, who seemed to be afraid of them. And the women brought in the majority of the sales so the old boys had good reason to bow down to them.

Still, I should not have stayed at this job. The long-term effects would be difficult, but at that point in my life, the perks, salary, benefits, car allowance, gas and corporate credit cards, and freedom outweighed the pitfalls. I learned how to stay out of the office most of the time. In fact, as long as I told them I was going on sales calls, no one really checked on my comings and goings.

These perks were exactly what a good friend had told me about when she encouraged me to take this job. She was one of those badass women I mentioned and knew very well how to work this system to her advantage. What I didn't bargain for when I found myself smack in the middle of this old boys' club was how good it would feel to be wrapped in the protection of a very strong network of women. One of these women became my soul friend, sister, mentor, role model, and one of the greatest gifts in my life.

Barbara and I met and bonded in that way only smokers can. After the first few times we saw each other outside smoking, we decided to take our breaks together. She would buzz my office, "Wanna go have a cigarette?" Sure. As our friendship grew, she would simply shoot me an email, "Ready?" Or I would stroll by her office and raise my eyebrows. The secret language of smokers is inclusive and masterful.

She was the company's marketing director and set up many new client meetings for the salespeople. She handled awkward cold calls, built relationships, and pulled together amazing samples and presentations for the sales staff to take to meetings with potential clients. She basically handed us sales on a silver platter. We only had to close the deal.

Since I was new, she was tasked with training and mentoring me. Initially, she attended meetings with me because she had arranged them and started to build trust and rapport with the potential client. Barbara has an aura that makes you feel as if you've known her for years. Additionally, she is gorgeous, charming, and brilliant.

We became somewhat of a dynamic duo in the old boys' world of printing since attractive saleswomen could usually count on a meeting and normally at least one job. Male clients liked to look at us and perhaps fantasize that maybe they could do more with us, so they gave us work to keep us coming back. In return, we treated them to great lunches and gave them our undivided attention for an hour or two. Sometimes, the printing jobs barely canceled out the money we spent on lunches, but that wasn't really our concern. They told us to sell, and we sold.

We may have manipulated our way into some sales from our male clients, but the truth was: We were girls' girls and developed relationships of mutual trust, respect, and ultimately friendship with our female clients. They gave us work because they knew we had their backs and would run interference and go to bat for them to make sure they were treated fairly by the company.

Over the course of a year, we smoked cartons of cigarettes, drank gallons of coffee, and traveled around Ohio and Pennsylvania, peddling our always charming selves and our printing wares.

When I first met Barbara, she'd recently been through a painful divorce and was positively skeletal. I once observed at the copy machine that her size zero skirt was pinned tighter so it wouldn't fall off of her tiny hips. On our very first road trip, we visited multiple leads, smoked many cigarettes, drank *a lot* of coffee but never stopped to eat. By late afternoon, I was faint and woozy from hunger and asked Barbara, who was driving, "Are we going to eat before we go back to the office?"

"Oh, are you hungry? We can stop. Food isn't a very big deal to me," she said as if the thought of food hadn't even crossed her mind. As I grew to know her better, I realized it had not.

We did stop, and after my lightheadedness subsided and I inhaled a burger, I said, "I really like you, and today was so much fun. But food is a really big deal to me, so if we are gonna travel together, can we please fit eating into our schedule?"

She laughed her delightful-with-a-touch-of-devious laugh and said, "Oh honey, you should have told me! Of course we can!" And from then on, we did. Usually, she ordered a coffee or maybe soup that she stirred around, sniffed and rarely ate, but she always made sure we stopped.

Although we were about the same height, 5'3", people often described Barbara as tall. Maybe because we she was rail thin and wore heels. Maybe because she had such a big personality and commanded the attention of every room she entered. I don't know. I still think of her as tall even when I see pictures of us being the same height.

During the road trips and smoke breaks and sometimes liquid lunches, we talked about everything under the sun. Our childhoods, mothers, fathers, sisters, boyfriends, husbands, exes, children—she had a teenage daughter, and at this time, I had a preteen daughter and toddler son—hopes, dreams, fears and more. In knowing her, I glimpsed who I wanted to be when I "grew up." I also found another sister relationship like the one I'd always wanted and, ultimately, the mother I hoped to be.

She was raising her daughter to be a strong and independent woman. Although she was a single mother, and her daughter was an only child, she maintained a great relationship with her daughter's father and his family. Additionally, she surrounded them both with a loving, supportive clan of grandparents, step-grandparents, aunts and uncles.

She introduced me to all sorts of concepts I'd never experienced. Spirituality and mediums for example. We took several trips to Lilydale, the world's largest center for spiritualism and mediums, where we had readings, drank wine, and discussed philosophy with some of the most brilliant people I've ever met. Years later, we took our daughters back to this magical place and drank bellinis, laughed, smoked and were the coolest moms on the planet, at least in our own self-congratulatory assessment.

We read books by some great thought leaders together—Carolyn Myss, Marianne Williamson, Debbie Ford, Gary Zukav. For one whole month we delved into finding our archetypes as we devoured Carolyn Myss' *Sacred Contracts*. We emailed back and forth all day from our offices that were about twenty-five steps apart.

As the end of my first year of employment neared, it became clear that the company was headed for closure. Barbara was proactive and found another job before our printing ship hit the iceberg. I didn't say goodbye to her on her last day because I was so emotionally distraught at the prospect of losing her. When I came in the first morning after she left, a medallion of the Virgin Mary hung on my computer with a note that said, "I won't be here to protect you, but I think she will do okay." With that sweet gesture, she healed a part of that little girl inside me who desperately longed to be protected.

Although I feared our friendship wouldn't endure the loss of that common workplace—traveling and smoking and using comic relief to survive the day-to-day drudgery—our continuing closeness proved that it was not a reason or season of friendship but one that would last a lifetime. We continue to grow and change, sometimes not seeing each other or talking for months but instantly picking right back up as if we'd never been separated.

We quit smoking. Our girls grew up and became friends. My whole family attended her wedding to the guy she had divorced when we first met—but that's her story to tell. When her daughter found her own happily ever after, Chloe and I accompanied them to pick out her wedding dress, just as we'd planned years earlier in Lilydale. We celebrated her daughter's wedding with her family, and I'm certain she'll be there to celebrate our children's weddings with us.

She is one of the smartest women I have ever known, and I'm a much better person for her influence in my life. We shared a common missing mother energy—mothers that fell short, were envious, did some really horrific things. We shared a mutual adoration for our silly and unconventional dads. She lost her mom. We both lost our dads. She bears that non-judgmental attitude that only comes from having lived and experienced all manner of hard shit in your life. She is a shining example of, "You aren't what happens to you." And that is exactly what I needed to see. No matter what was going on in my life or what was coming up from my past, she would listen and help me try to reframe it and uncover the lesson life was trying to teach me.

Once, after a series of unfortunate events that led to the end of another friendship. I had a hard time wrapping my head around what happened and found myself sharing details with her. I felt betrayed, sad, hurt, and she was the very first person to introduce to me to the concept that what happened had absolutely nothing to do with me. This person, my friend, had been going through a midlife revolution, and instead of offering her compassion and support, I'd taken her actions as a personal affront and distanced myself from her when she really needed a friend the most.

"It's not about you," Barbara advised. "It's not about anyone but her."

She was the first person I knew who came from a fucked-up childhood, a less than perfect family and overcame it to be a really great mom and a fantastic person. Just by living her life exactly how she did, she gave me hope that I too could turn out to be a good mom, a good person, and a functioning member of society, even though I didn't have a great relationship with my family of origin. Even though I'd suffered traumas. Even though I'd lost siblings to drugs and suicide. Those things happened *to* me; they didn't have to define the person I was or the person I could become.

On December 1, 2015, my beautiful friend called to tell me she had been diagnosed with lung cancer. All of our fucking cigarette breaks come to pass like this. Still, I had no doubt in my mind that she would kick cancer right in the balls like she did the one creepy executive who pushed her a bit too far. And she did. But it shook me to my very core to think that my friend—my strong, beautiful, invincible, amazing girl—could even face something so worldly, so base as cancer. I've always envisioned her as a creature not quite of this earth... an energy stopping by, but far too divine to stay. She functions in her own plane that's a little bit between here and heaven, and I'm grateful for every moment I get to spend with her.

The universe really showed up, bringing Barbara into my life. She has been the answer to so many prayers and a real-life spirit guide wrapped in a tiny, gorgeous, wise-cracking package.

CHAPTER 7:
WHAT IF YOU TAKE OFF YOUR MASK AND THEY LOVE YOU ANYWAY?

"To be nobody but myself in a world which is doing its best, night and day, to make me somebody else means to fight the hardest battle any human can fight, and never stop fighting."

—*E. E. Cummings*

"Everything will line up perfectly when knowing and living the truth becomes more important than looking good."

—*Alan Cohen*

WHAT MY MOM COULDN'T communicate through chocolate chips, meatloaves, and rosaries, she did through silence and notes. Often, the first indication that she was upset with you was silence. Once, when I was twelve, the indication took the form of dirty clothes. Since the washer and dryer were directly next to the kitchen and they were always running, I realized within a pretty reasonable amount of time that she was in fact washing clothes. She was just not washing mine.

I inquired, "Mom, can you wash my clothes? I don't have any clean clothes."

Without breaking her concentration on the cookie dough she stirred or making eye contact, she said, "You can do your own laundry from now on. I'm sick and tired of you keeping your room like a pig sty and then throwing clean clothes in the hamper." She listed a few more offenses, but I really only heard that I needed to learn how to do laundry in a hurry. I pulled this memory out several times when my own children put clean clothes into their hamper instead of putting them away. "You know," I admonished them, "When I did this, Nanny made me do my own laundry.

Another time, in eighth grade, I realized that she was mad at me when a bikini that I had coveted, saved for, and finally bought with my own money went missing. After searching everywhere with no results, I asked my mom if she had seen it.

Again without eye contact, "I took it."

"Why?"

"Because you are a disrespectful snot."

"What did I do?"

A list of offenses followed. Back talk, smart mouthing, being a pig, pretty typical teenage assholery, but chiefly among these grievous transgressions was daring to have an opinion that didn't agree with hers, and even worse, voicing it.

"I bought it with my own money, so it isn't yours to take. Please give it back."

Shockingly, that assertion didn't go over well. My bikini remained missing for several more weeks until she completed a multi-page contract. That's right, she typed (on an old-fashioned typewriter with actual carbon paper copies) a multi-page contract, complete with a line for me to initial after every one of her rules. The list included:

"I will not to talk back to my mother."

"I will keep my room neat and orderly."

"I will do my laundry weekly and wash only clothes that have actually been on my body for a reasonable period of time and not stuff clean clothes in my hamper because I am a lazy pig."

When I think about my self-talk now, I realize that my inner critic sounds just like my mother communicating to my teenage self.

Once I initialed and signed the manifesto, I got my bikini back, learned a valuable lesson in laundry, and learned to smile to her face and say and do what I wanted behind her back. Unfortunately, her tough love didn't teach me to be respectful; it taught me to be sneaky.

When I was a cheerleader in high school, she accompanied me to a "Parents' Night" celebration. It was one of those events where players and cheerleaders are introduced and walk across the field with their parents or other escorts. On our way to the field, I passed a girl that I wasn't really friends with and about whom another friend and I had recently been talking. We said hi and kept walking.

My mother vice-gripped my arm digging her pointy fingernails into my bicep as she whispered through clenched teeth: "You make me sick. You are the most two-faced, disgusting human being I have ever encountered, and I am ashamed to be your mother." Then, she released her grip and looped her arm through mine, smiling and waving as we were introduced.

What she didn't realize, and I did, is that I was becoming a much better protégé than she realized. I was becoming not who the person she desperately coerced me into being, but the person she was at her worst—catty and phony.

My dad was usually the one who dished out physical abuse, and my mom rarely hit me other than an occasional slap here and there. The last time she tried to slap me, I was eighteen. She was taking me to school very early in the morning for a choir trip to Chicago. A full-blown but fairly disorganized smoker at this point, I needed to buy cigarettes for the trip—because a school trip required a lot of cigarettes. Although she knew I smoked, when I asked her to stop at the gas station so I could buy cigarettes, she refused.

Frustrated at the prospect of being without cigarettes for three days, I muttered under my breath, "You're such a bitch." She swung her hand to slap me, but I caught it. We stared at each other for a few long seconds. When I got out of the car, our relationship had taken a different turn. Knowing that I was physically stronger and no longer afraid of her, she ramped up the psychological and emotional control tactics.

That evening, she made her feelings clear when I called collect—it was 1991—from Chicago to tell her we had arrived safely, and she refused to accept the call. I called my boyfriend's mother, who then called my mom to inform her I'd arrived safely. My mother gushed, "Oh, thank goodness you've heard from her. I've been worried sick."

Still in the midst of the passive-aggressiveness, she dished out enough of her own brand of love to keep me coming back for more. Additionally, I began subconsciously sending "Are you my mother?" energy out into the world. As it is wont to do, the universe responded with mother after mother after mother.

It took me a long time to realize what exactly was going on. It took me even longer to recognize the women right in front of me who mended my broken spirit and helped me find joy and purpose. I didn't have to settle for the person who'd brought my body into the world when the universe provided so many others who *chose* to love me even though they didn't have to.

Although I learned a multitude of lessons from the conditional love I received in my family of origin, I missed out on the vital gift of unconditional love. In our house, love was earned, not doled out just because you existed. You performed to get love. Achieve, excel, behave, smile, be skinny, be pretty, do not say inappropriate things, etc. Basically, I learned to be someone else in order to get the temporary approval that stood in for love. And then, it was another experience to learn how to give unconditional love and accept it when it was offered.

I actually learned that I had the capacity to give it when I had my first child, Chloe. Most mothers agree that children can't really do anything to make their mother stop loving them. However, it's easier to give unconditional love to our children than it is to others.

And I didn't get many examples of unconditional love in my family of origin. We were estranged from a good part of my dad's family. My mom didn't like his mother. They didn't speak to his brother, but the only real motivation for that seemed to be a story about said brother's wife attempting to get my dad fired from his job. It wasn't something anyone talked about much, but my mom had a knack for subtle and outright manipulation as well as performing underhanded tasks to get her way. At one point, she turned Chris in to the police for drug possession. She accused Brian of stealing from her—

which no one ever really believed he did—to get my dad to agree to change the locks to keep him from coming to their house. Basically, if being estranged from my dad's family was her goal, she would have found a way to achieve it.

Then they didn't speak to my dad's youngest brother because they didn't approve of how he treated his kids. Then they barely spoke to his oldest brother because my mom found his daughter to be obnoxious.

For years, my brother and sister didn't speak because of their own disagreements. My brother didn't get to see my nephews and niece until shortly before his death.

My mother still nurses barely-below-the-surface rage and a nearly thirty-year grudge against my former sister-in-law for her behavior on a visit my mom describes as "the weekend from hell." Among said sister-in-law's transgressions were that she wasn't appropriately appreciative of my mother's grocery shopping and cooking even though she (the sister-in-law) "didn't have any food in the house."

In my family of origin, having differences of opinion or arguments or fights meant cutting people out of your life. No one sat down to discuss problems. No one agreed to disagree. If someone made you mad, you were done with them. If you disagreed with someone, you didn't address issues or try to get past it, you simply washed your hands of the person and pretended they never existed. Except in the case of the aforementioned sister-in-law where my mom typed a scathing, single-spaced, two-page letter citing all the sister-in-law's wrongdoings. Again, complete with an actual carbon paper copy.

I learned to walk away instead of trying to understand another's perspective or accept other people's flaws and shortcomings. My mom didn't seem capable of self-reflection and never entertained the idea that her own flaws and shortcomings could cause conflict. For many years, I followed this same pattern. I walked away from friends and family because of hurt feelings and offenses.

But while I knew how to walk away from people, I quickly realized that I was incapable of turning off my feelings. It's pointless to walk away if you just continue the relationship in your mind. I'll go over and over every conversation, every action, every thought, and ruminate to the brink of insanity. So, it crossed my mind that maybe cutting people out of my life wasn't the best approach to handling conflict. Maybe it was worthwhile to have conversations. Perhaps we could try to work through our differences. Maybe it was even okay to allow others to own their behavior, own my own, and agree to disagree.

In this endeavor, I had a great teacher. My husband's aunt Susie is one hundred percent authentically who she is. She is one of the kindest, most loving people I've ever known; however, she is not afraid to tell someone what she thinks. She loves the people around her more fully and truly than anyone I've ever known, and from the moment I met her, she seemed to get me in a way few others did. I know that many other people in the world feel exactly the same way about her because she is one of those rare human beings who takes the time to know, understand, and love people.

She accepts each person she meets right where they are, but that doesn't stop her from encouraging them to become better—the best—versions of themselves. Honestly, if love alone was enough to change people, she would singlehandedly be responsible for many amazing transformations.

Observing her love the people in her life so genuinely and unconditionally has taught me an amazing lesson. You don't have to agree with people to love them. You don't have to understand people to love them. You can disagree with their choices and still love them. You can call people out on their bad behavior and still love them. You can be disappointed over and over by people and still love them. You can be who you genuinely are, even if the people around you decide not to live their best lives.

Watching Susie taught me that it's possible to show up in every moment as your authentic self, and if that means having uncomfortable conversations, that's what you do. If it means telling someone lovingly but clearly that they are being an asshole, you can do that. And if it means reaching out to say, "Hey, be extra careful today because I had a dream you were in a car accident," as she did a few times to me, then you do that too. Even if someone thinks you're crazy, it doesn't matter when you do that from a place of love, as she always, always does.

I learned, observing her over the years, how to negotiate different types of relationships, from difficult friendships to adult children and in-law issues. I learned how to give advice—when someone asked for it—without sounding condescending or preachy. I'm still learning to negotiate new and different hardships along my journey, but she is always available for advice, a pep talk, or an honest, loving opinion.

Some people don't value the truth-tellers in their lives. In fact, many people would prefer Susie keep her mouth shut and not shed any light on the phoniness, selfishness, and dysfunctionality that permeate their lives. But I adore the truth-tellers. I want to live the most authentic life I can. Bullshit, small talk, and phoniness make my skin crawl. I spent too much of my life pretending everything was okay while it was really a big simmering shit stew, and I absolutely refuse to pretend for another minute.

Although I am extremely grateful for the model Susie sets, I've drawn tighter boundaries. While I no longer feel the need to cut people out of my life, that doesn't mean that everyone has full access to me. I keep the people who have repeatedly hurt me at arm's length. Many people don't value the difference between real and superficial anyway, so as long as you smile at them and speak kindly on the occasions you interact, the relationship can remain pleasant.

And there is no hard and fast rule that says we need to have great relationships with people simply because we share DNA. Choose who to spend time with. Let your friends become your chosen family. Cherish those who love you not because of some sense of duty or obligation but because they see, appreciate, love, and accept you. Because you bring value to their lives and they want to be part of yours. These people are your family. You don't have to get caught up in an outdated definition of this word. If what you define as family doesn't work, then redefine it.

My definition is this: A group of people who mutually love, support, and encourage each other. People you can count on. People who show up for celebrations and tragedies. Your tribe.

Find them. Love them. Never let them go.

CHAPTER 8:
DYING A THOUSAND DEATHS

"Do the best you can until you know better. Then when you know better, do better."

—*Maya Angelou*

IT IS THROUGH NO special selection process that a sibling gets his own chapter. It's very simple: Those who lived can tell their own stories.

I've read that when a person commits suicide he or she dies once, but those left behind die a thousand times. Day after week after month, they die, rehashing conversations, questioning interactions, suppressing overwhelming guilt over unkind words or thoughts. Asking why, wondering if they could have prevented it, analyzing conversations for signs they might have missed. All this over and over and over until you're crazy. Yes, those left behind suffer long after our lost loved one's pain has subsided.

My brother Brian was the fifth born child, and the last child of the "first family." My first five siblings were born in about as many years. Then there was a five-year gap before my closest brother, Rich, and I joined the party. Brian was a clown. Next to Chris, he was the brother I was closest to, both in proximity and emotion. He had a great sense of humor, but we learned later that he used it mostly as a defense mechanism to cover up the pain he carried. Our oldest nephew nicknamed him "Uncle Balky," and it stuck for the rest of his life.

Balky unarguably suffered the worst of my dad's wrath. My father was mercilessly tough on my gentle, freckled brother. Sometimes, when I think about it, I can't rationalize loving a person who treated his own child so horribly, but I've compartmentalized this, enabling me to love my dad despite how he destroyed my brother. He called him a liar, criticized, berated, and condemned him. Nothing Balky did measured up to my dad's lofty expectations from the time he was a little boy, and he nearly always took the blame for anything that had been broken, moved, lost, or misplaced.

One of my dad's oft-screamed phrases was, "Keep your hands off things that don't belong to you." But in a house filled with seven children, no one kept their hands off anything. Especially not a mini-orange tree that was one of my father's favorite things to freak out about us not keeping our hands off. To this day, one mention of "that fucking orange tree" elicits a collective groan. Someone was always getting into trouble for orange-tree-related incidents. My sister used to use little branches that had broken off to dig in the dirt while chatting on the phone in our upstairs hallway. When I first divulged this information to my brothers, they jumped on it like it was the most valuable scoop ever uttered. How do you know? Did she tell you? When did you see her?

Quite simply, the fact that my sister found me annoying and didn't want me anywhere around her made her exceptionally fascinating. So I studied her from afar and spied on her every chance I got.

Once, when I was about four or five, Balky took a severe beating for breaking a branch on the orange tree. I crept into his room, and he was crying. My older brothers never cried and admonished me not to be a wimp whenever I did. Seeing him cry made me feel extremely protective, even though he was eight years older. Not knowing how to fix things, I crawled up next to him and wrapped my little arms around him. Normally, he would have shoved me away and pretended not to cry, but that particular night, he just lay there.

About sixteen years later, we replayed that scene one night, as I climbed into bed with him, grateful he was alive after a drug and drinking binge that had him missing for a few days. That time, I cried because I couldn't protect him, and I couldn't fix anything for him.

When he was in first grade, he set a garbage can on fire at school. No one seems particularly clear on the details of this rebellious act. My dad not only beat him, but he shaved his head. This was in the late 1960s early 1970s when boys often wore their hair long, and my mom said that he had been growing his hair out for some time. This punishment went beyond discipline and extended into intentional humiliation. Once, in a rare moment of self-reflection, my mother said that she wished she had never told my dad what Balky did.

When Chris died, I think Balky saw an opportunity for redemption. Chris was my dad's unabashed favorite son, and with him gone, a slot opened. By this point, our three other remaining brothers had headed off in different directions around the country, fleeing the Swan curse, I think. Balky tried to fill Chris' shoes with my dad. Hanging out and watching movies, going golfing, doing things that my dad enjoyed doing, and mostly just being with him. Although my dad developed a better relationship with Balky in later years, I don't think he ever felt my dad's approval.

He lived with my parents longer than any of us. Even after he'd gotten married, fights with his wife and drug binges brought him back to my parents' house. By his early thirties, his drug use seemed to be spiraling out of control, and we planned an intervention. Unfortunately, it was foiled when someone told his wife our plans, and she told him. He called and screamed at me, saying he was fine and who the fuck did we think we were anyway.

There are some hurts that are so deep that you have to physically force yourself to deal with them. There isn't enough alcohol or cocaine or crack to numb them. The only way to truly get through that kind of pain is to submerge yourself and hope you can swim through it without drowning. Heartbreakingly, he wasn't able to do that. The last time I talked to him, he had his mask firmly in place, laughing and joking and telling me he was going back to school to be a chiropractor. I eagerly swallowed every lie he told me, believing what I wanted so desperately to be true. Years later, in graduate school, I learned that I had missed a big sign of suicide. When a previously depressed person all of a sudden seems to be positive and excited about the future, sometimes it is because they've formulated a plan to end their pain, which has given them that elusive sense of peace.

The day he died was like any other day. Actually, I don't know what the day he died was like. The day they *found* him was like any other day. I hadn't woken up with any bad feelings in my stomach. No deep gurgling that told me something bad was going to happen. It felt like a normal Tuesday.

It was hot. August. Our best friends were getting married that weekend, and Brad and I were both in the wedding. My parents' fortieth anniversary was the following weekend, and our three out-of-state brothers were flying in for a surprise party we had planned. My favorite times are those when I have lots of fun things to look forward to, so this was a great week.

At that time, I worked at a small print shop around the corner from my parents' home, and they babysat Chloe who was three. Every day, I spent my lunch hour at their house loving on my baby girl as my mom filled me in on their day.

That Tuesday, I was eating a tuna salad sandwich, and Chloe was sitting in her high chair, coloring and telling me about their trip to K-Mart when the phone rang. I watched my mom scurry around the kitchen, looking for something—a phone book. *What is she doing?* She sat down at the table muttering, "Mmm hmmm. Yes. Mmm hmmm. Okay, Peach will come."

My anxiety level increased, and as she flipped through the phone book, I scanned the names upside down, wondering what she searched for so intently. Feeling my eyes on her, she looked up at me and mouthed, "Balky killed himself," just as my eyes landed on McCardell-White—the name of the funeral home at the end of the street where we would now be viewing yet another brother's body.

My brother killed himself. I leaped up and promptly vomited my not-yet-digested lunch into the garbage can. I walked out the back door and called Brad at work. "Come to Porter Street, please. Balky killed himself." Brad always asks a million questions, but this particular day, I had nothing but a million questions in return. No one ever answered them.

In the midst of this confusion was my tiny little girl watching her mom fall apart. My tiny little girl, who told her daddy, "Mommy's cwying cuz Uncle Balky shooted hisself," when he arrived. Years later, she would tell me she was afraid to go to his funeral because he was being cremated. In her baby mind, she pieced together that we were all going to watch her beloved uncle get burned up.

The days following were a blur. The next few years, actually, were a blur. Brad asked, "What's wrong?" so many times that I finally screamed, "MY BROTHER KILLED HIMSELF! THAT'S WHAT'S WRONG! AND UNTIL FURTHER NOTICE THAT'S WHAT'S GOING TO BE WRONG!" I felt helpless. I tried to protect him. I tried to save him. I tried to make him feel loved and important, but I couldn't.

Part of me holds on to pain like one holds on to the memory of how to do something that you don't do often but you might need to perform quickly someday. For instance, if you haven't jumped rope in years, it feels kind of creaky and awkward at first, but soon, your body remembers, and it feels easy and natural.

When Chris died, it felt as if my whole world fell apart. Once, when I was a little girl, I backed into an electric fence, which felt like being kicked by a horse. In fact, I turned around to look for a horse. Chris' death felt similar, except the kick knocked out my stomach, leaving me walking around with a gaping hole in my center. I could feel the wind blowing through the place where my soul used to reside. When Balky died, that pain rushed right back, carving new wounds through my body while it ripped open old ones. While there were unanswered questions, this time, there were no conspiracy theories. Instead, there was a stack of Post-its telling the sad details of my brother's hopeless desperation.

Pain is like my hometown. It isn't where I live now, but when I go back there, I recognize nearly everything. Sure, some new buildings have been built, and a couple stores have been closed or re-opened as new businesses. The fast food restaurant is a coffee shop, the shoe store is an antique dealer, and so forth, but it's all pretty much the same. I feel comfortable here. I know my way around. Some of the faces have changed, but it feels pretty much the same.

Death hurts. Suicide hurts worse. Dealing with the surprise and the overwhelming sadness and the stupid questions is debilitating. People said, "Suicide is selfish. Aren't you mad at him?" How could I be mad at someone who already hated himself that much? I was mad at my own inability to make him feel loved enough to want to live. I was mad at my dad for beating him, crushing his spirit, and never making him feel good enough. I was mad at my mom for practicing tough love with a person who was so fragile that he needed the most tender, caring, nurturing affection. I was mad that we failed him. I was mad that the world failed him. I wasn't mad at him.

I felt physically sick imagining Balky so sad and desperate and feeling as if he had nowhere to turn. The fact that we were here and loved him was not enough. The thought of his sadness overwhelming his coping mechanisms, waves of depression washing away the lifelines we held, nearly destroyed me.

Once my dad mused that Balky "just couldn't shake those demons," and I realized he was clueless about the demons he had given us. My dad thought he was making us tough, making us better people. In reality, he broke our spirits. What we grow up with definitely shapes who we become, but it doesn't have to perpetuate a cycle of bad behavior. My dad was mentally and physically abused by his father, who shot himself when he was in his sixties. His father probably had a pretty rough upbringing himself. My dad carried on that cycle, not knowing any better. And that cycle proved to be too much for two of my brothers. I look around all the time and see people living out how they were raised, repeating cycles. It's easier to do what we were taught and far more difficult to pave our own way.

I have tried with all my strength to sow love, compassion, and acceptance into my children. I have read countless books because I didn't feel my parents sowed those qualities into us as children. Many of us didn't have the benefit of parents who had dealt with their own stuff. Maybe your parents beat, abused, ignored, or belittled you. Maybe instead of being your safe place, your dad was the source of your fear. Maybe instead of being the person who made all your problems better, your mom made you feel like a failure.

If you consider the people who knock you down, you'll probably find that they are acting out of their own suffering. Perhaps your boss who is overly critical of your work, seeing only the mistakes, was raised by a mother who never acknowledged the stories she wrote when she was a little girl and only pointed out the misspelled words. At any given point, we can change our own or someone else's story by choosing love.

For a long time, I carried tremendous guilt for having survived my family of origin. Why did I make it when my brothers didn't? I also felt that I needed to do something really important with this gift of life. The guilt and extreme pressure kept me in a prison of my own making. It took me quite a while to realize that I didn't need to save the world, I just needed to love people. I couldn't save my brothers. I couldn't change my parents. I can't fix anything for anyone, but I can love. I can listen. I can empathize. And as long as I can, I will.

CHAPTER 9:
BLOOD IS NOT ALWAYS THICKER THAN WATER

"Friends are the family we choose for ourselves."
—Edna Buchanan

THE BOYS I CHOSE to love in my life—I say 'boys' because I fell in love for the last time when I was seventeen and he was sixteen—had families that I was drawn to almost as much as I was drawn to the boys. The first boy had a very strong, confident, loving and protective mom. She was one of the most genuine women I've ever known and remains someone I love and admire to this day. Nearly thirty years after we were part of each other's lives, she holds part of my heart. Each time I lost someone I loved, and each time I gave birth to a new person to love, she showed up. There's a connection between our hearts that couldn't be severed.

When my brother Chris died, and my house felt confusing, dishonest, and volatile, she scooped me up and took me to her house where no one was sad or crying or whispering, and everything felt safe for a little while. I'll never forget the kindness she showed me, and I wonder now if the reason I was drawn to that particular boy was so that his mom could walk beside me and sometimes carry me through that terrible time in my life. The universe works in strange and mysterious ways to provide for our well-being.

I also fell in love with the next boy's mother—who would become my mother-in-law—but for very different reasons. She was not strong or confident or particularly protective, but she was soft and kind and sentimental. She created many sweet traditions in her family that I found charming and endearing. They visited amusement parks and water parks and zoos. Unlike our family who got there at opening, hit the best rides, ate our packed lunches and left, the Bells drained every last bit of fun out their experiences. They arrived at park opening just like my family, but they rode every. Single. Ride. Visited every. Single. Kiosk. Shopped at every. Single. Store. And they were always among the last people to leave the park at closing time.

They took surprise family trips to look at Christmas lights. They detoured off the vacation path to see kitschy attractions like hot air balloon launches or antique malls. If they saw a sign that looked interesting, they checked it out. They never had a firm agenda; instead, they rolled along like tumbleweeds blown in the direction of their curiosity.

I found all of this magical. My future husband found it miserable.

My mother-in-law had a childlike enthusiasm for life that I found delightful since my own mother was rigid and glued to beliefs and rituals. There were no unplanned detours on trips. You stopped at the same rest stops. You ate the same food. You wore the same clothes. You didn't deviate from the routine. Why? "Because this is how we do it." There was no such thing as changing, adapting, making things better. You just do what you always did.

Holding tightly to some sort of routine, exercising a small bit of control and predictability in a life where things often fell apart and people often got angry and sometimes died makes sense to me now. Then, it just felt boring.

My future mother-in-law was as spontaneous as my own mom was regimented. During the first years Brad and I dated, she happily enveloped me into their family and included me in their traditions. The first summer we were together, I accompanied them to Disney World. It was a long drive to Florida, especially after their station wagon's air conditioning died less than halfway into the trip. Still, we stopped at rest areas and had picnics, detoured into a motel for a swim and overnight sleep. We even got off the highway at the first beach we saw when we got to Florida. Brad and I and his two younger sisters raced to the ocean and got sweaty, salty, and sandy while she laughed and took 7000 pictures. It was nothing like any trip I'd ever been on in my life, and I had the *best* time.

For Christmas, she invited me to make cookies and rock candy with her. She also invited me on shopping trips with her and her girlfriend once a month as they frequented outlet stores and went to dinner. The first Christmas I spent with them, she gave me a handmade ornament, a tradition that she had with her own kids. It felt a lot like having the mom I'd always dreamed of.

We had a great relationship for several years. In fact, it only started to sour when I was eight months pregnant with Chloe. Brad and I were college students, nineteen and twenty, living at our respective homes with our respective parents when I got pregnant. We were barely ready to be adults and certainly not ready to be parents at the time. However, nothing gives you the impetus to grow up like a life growing inside of you that you'll soon be responsible for. My mother decided that I could do my growing up somewhere else and told me I was not welcome to live in their home anymore after the baby came. With very little money and fewer choices, I begrudgingly moved in with my future in-laws.

The end of my pregnancy, the time that we spent living with Brad's parents, and the next ten years or so felt like an episode of *Everybody Loves Raymond,* or in other words, an in-law nightmare. It started with my mother-in-law pointing out in the delivery room that seeing my baby was just like "giving birth to Bradley all over again" and that if she hadn't seen my pregnant belly—and c-section scar—she would have never even guessed I had anything to do with my baby. The relationship deteriorated over the years to the point that we didn't speak for a year.

During that silent year, I got an unexpected blessing in the form of my friend and soul sister Julia. Julia and I met on an oprah.com message board called "Dealing with Your In-Laws." For a long time, we knew each other only by our screen names, Julia was "What Now" and I was "DIL [daughter-in-law] In Distress."

At the beginning of our friendship, we were on complete opposite sides of the coin. Julia was the mother-in-law learning to navigate new territory with her adult children, their spouses and significant others, and grandchildren. I was looking for validation, wondering if everyone dealt with similar issues, and mostly looking for a place to vent. In fact, I remember vividly that our first interaction consisted of my projecting a whole lot of crap onto her by virtue of verbally attacking her in the comments of one of her posts. Because she was a mature and enlightened human, she naturally saw through my projection and called me on it in a loving and compassionate manner. From this shaky ground, we began a very open dialogue. She told me about her own in-law issues, and I told her about mine. We corresponded on the site for a long while before moving on to talking through email and eventually phone, text, and Facebook. Although we only met once in person, I feel as if I know her and she knows me better than many of my family members. We were each other's long-distance best friends.

Knowing Julia helped me to see my mother-in-law from a different perspective. Julia had similar traditions with her children. She wanted her family all around for every holiday, birthday, and special occasion—and she made every occasion very special. What I had often seen as my mother-in-law's attempts to control, I saw only as love in Julia, and it helped me re-frame many things in my own life.

Despite identifying with the plight of the oft-attacked "monster-in-law," Julia supported me wholeheartedly when my mother-in-law said or did thoughtless or insensitive things. One of my biggest triggers was my mother-in-law's constant comparison of every minute detail about my children to my husband, one of his sisters, herself, her family, my father-in-law, and basically anyone but me. She once laughingly told me, "People tell me all the time it doesn't look like you had anything to do with my grandchildren." It was as if she was adamant to prove the children did not carry any of my DNA, and it felt hurtful and infuriating.

For example, I have blonde hair and blue eyes. My husband has black hair and brown eyes. Our kids all have brown eyes, which they obviously get from their dad, and they all had blonde hair when they were little. If someone mentioned that one of our children had my hair in her presence, she would immediately counter with, "Bradley had blond hair when he was little too." When Chloe was an early reader, she quickly attributed that to my sister-in-law. "Oh, she gets that from Lisa. Lisa read early." The fact that I was reading *American Heiress*—the true story of Patty Hearst's kidnapping—when I was seven was irrelevant. The fact that my mother, a former English teacher had been reading to Chloe and doing phonics with her since she was three was also irrelevant. It was those strong Bell genes that made her a reader.

The constant hurtful comparisions went on and on. When Chloe called me "mama," she had obviously inherited that from my sister-in-law who had called *her* mama. She had feet just like one sister-in-law. Small bones like my mother-in-law—which triggered my own insecurity about my big bones. Her eyes were the exact same color as my father-in-law's. Her temper was from my mother-in-law's brother. Her fingernails were very white like my mother-in-law's.

It felt overwhelming and hurtful. I thought that this woman loved me, so it felt like a bitter betrayal that she didn't want anything about my kids to be like me. If I was a worthwhile person, why would it be bad for my kids to inherit things from me? Sometimes, in moments of desperate vulnerability, I remarked on particular things about the kids that were like me. I thought maybe she just didn't know that much about me; surely if she did, she would agree. But that was not the case. Instead, she would immediately refute any of my claims saying, "Oh, no she gets that from (insert member of my husband's family)."

But Chloe was attached to my hip, my tiny BFF, so it eased the sting of the comments immensely. Then our beautiful baby boy, Peyton, arrived and he had big blonde curls exactly like mine when I was a baby. Finally, I thought. No one in their family has one bit of texture to their hair. Finally, I can claim something that she can't possibly give anyone else credit for.

Well, you already know that things wouldn't work out that simply for me, right? My mother-in-law would say over and over, "I wonder where he gets those curls?" I would answer, "From me." Ignoring me, she would continue to muse, "Well, my niece has curly hair, it might be from her." Her niece had curly hair because her father—who shared no DNA with my children—had curly hair. I would point that out, and she would ignore me. Once she acknowledged me but only to snap, "Your hair is wavy, but it isn't curly." I shared this ongoing saga with Julia. She said, "Send me a picture of you when you were Peyton's age." So I did, and she promptly made him a batch of t-shirts with my baby picture on the front, showing beyond a reasonable doubt where he got his curls.

She was my lifeline when I thought I was certainly going to disappear or drown in the sea of invisibility. She saw me. She heard me. She told me I mattered. In addition to the in-law stuff, she also had navigated a complicated relationship with her mother and recommended some of the best books I've ever read regarding mother-daughter relationships. We bonded instantly, talking about books, families, husbands, our love of writing and creating. Honestly, we talked about everything. I shared things with her that I'd never told another soul, and in return, she offered honest, loving support.

Even when I did things she didn't agree with, she would lovingly point out to me what I was doing. She never judged or condemned me. She never walked away. When I look at how our lives have changed now, I feel overwhelmed with pride that we have both realized a lot of the dreams we supported each other through dreaming. She's living out many things we talked about all those years ago, and so am I. I will cherish her and our friendship forever.

As for my mother-in-law, we get along well now. It's been a long uphill battle, but I feel comfortable with the relationship we have, even though—shockingly—it's not the one I wanted. It was a lot of lessons in: You can't change another person. You can't change how someone else treats you. However, you can change yourself and how you react to it. I know now that my mother-in-law was only trying to cultivate connection and never to hurt my feelings or make me feel bad. It's never personal. Ultimately, she wanted the same love and acceptance I craved, but she sought it in a different way. Still, through those struggles came so many valuable lessons. And I'm forever grateful for the lifeline the universe sent me via oprah.com.

CHAPTER 10:
I GAVE BIRTH TO MY
GREATEST TEACHERS

"Children aren't ours to possess or own in any way. When we know this in the depths of our soul, we tailor our raising of them to their needs, rather than molding them to fit our needs."

—*Shefali Tsabary*

I SPENT A GOOD part of my thirties on a journey to self-improvement. Reading book after book, embracing my dark side, making friends with my shadow, naming my archetypes, forgiving, understanding, psychoanalyzing, and more, yet I still felt something was missing. I read about complicated sibling relationships, making friends with your mother, being a child of self-absorbed parents, and a whole library full of in-law books. I became a minor expert in narcissism because I felt that I was surrounded by narcissists.

When I was deeply involved in Christianity, I prayed, "God, show me who you want me to be. Help me be the person you put me here to be." But I saw nothing. Since I was raised to believe that God is perfect, and we are a mess, I assumed that God was showing me, and I was just too dense or inattentive or blonde to notice. I assumed the signs were there, and I just couldn't see or decipher them.

That is when I started to pray for God to be more obvious with His signs. My friend Barbara warned me, "You better be careful asking God to be more obvious. That's like opening Pandora's box."

I took her words with a grain of salt because when I asked God for additional clarity in His guidance, I imagined a prophetic dream or vision. You know, Old Testament, sun-standing-still stuff. I had romantic notions of a talking fox delivering wisdom without metaphors. Or maybe one of the birds of prey that liked to zoom at my head would drop something useful such as a counseling degree or the deed to a bookstore into my lap. Maybe a burning bush would spell out a message in clear if smoky letters in the sky.

As you can probably imagine, it didn't exactly happen like that. God, however, gave me a very clear message.

After we had our perfect family of one girl and one boy, and the old boys club printing company I'd worked for had closed its doors, I decided it was time to pursue a career that nourished my soul instead of just contributing to our checking account. Listening to people is one of my greatest gifts, so counseling seemed to be an ideal choice. Mental health professionals are in demand everywhere, so we wouldn't be stuck in Ohio. Additionally, I felt good about contributing positively to the world after too many years in soul-sucking sales positions.

Initially, everything fell into place very quickly and smoothly. I was accepted into a graduate program surrounded by peers who really felt like my tribe. The kind of people who respond, "Oh my gosh, me too!" the first time you share a crazy irrational fear with them and you realize, "Yes, these are my people." I had a whole group of them. All the classes were at night, so I didn't have to worry about childcare since Brad would be home with the kids. I was able to get financial aid, and after excelling in my classes for a few semesters, I got an assistantship that paid my tuition *and* gave me a stipend. Everything was coming up roses. I felt that I was exactly where I should be. Thank you, God.

Then, halfway to my degree, I started to feel bad, physically ill. I was tired all the time and constantly nauseated. I started to forget the most mundane daily tasks. Once I was so tired, I slept through a program at Peyton's school where I was supposed to be volunteering. I wasn't sure what was wrong, but in my head, it could be an undiagnosed illness or worse. A trip to the drug store confirmed that it was worse. In fact, it confirmed my worst fear: I was pregnant. Counseling was not in my immediate future because I saw no way to start a new career with a new baby. In fact, any career seemed impossible right at that moment, since I could barely stay awake through my classes, much less study. How could I possibly do an internship? We just finished paying for daycare; we definitely could not afford to start again when I didn't have a job.

How am I going to take care of another baby? We live in a three-bedroom house. I just got rid of all my baby stuff. Our kids are eleven and five; they're going to be so mad at me. In my mind, this pregnancy felt like a divinely placed roadblock right in the path of my counseling career. I was definitely *not* supposed to finish graduate school.

To complicate this, several of our very good friends were happily pregnant or nursing their much wanted, hoped for, and prayed for first children, and they were oh-so-happy for us. I wasn't happy. To be honest, I wanted to hurl myself down the nearest flight of stairs.

Although I can say now, from the safe and always wise perspective of hindsight: I don't really think professional counseling was my calling. If I'd stayed and finished, I might have been a good counselor, but I'm glad—now—that I bailed. That's now. At the time, I stormed around like a pouty two-year-old. Not my best performance.

Nothing is wasted, and I remain incredibly grateful for my experience in graduate school, the people I met, and the knowledge I gained. Maybe sitting in an office spending sixty-minute segments with people would not have been the right gig for me. I am certain I would have had a very difficult time not breaking down in tears of empathy and bringing people's problems home with me at night. One of my professors said once, when I asked her how counselors ever learned to keep professional distance, "You just get so used to things after a while, they no longer affect you." While I wanted that at the time, now, I realize, compassion and empathy are two of my best qualities. I didn't want to risk losing those if being compassionate and empathic was my job.

I certainly don't assert that our youngest child's conception was simply a divine roadblock to keep me from becoming a counselor. That kid has a purpose way beyond me. She is a wonderful warrior spirit and will likely accomplish things I couldn't have dreamed up. Also, I have a lot of quit in me, so I just need a tiny suggestion of a nudge to drop out of things. And I do use a lot of the skills I learned in grad school on a daily basis, when I listen to friends, family, and even people in line to pick up their kids at school. I am not a counselor by trade, but I do believe I offer service to people in need without an appointment, health insurance, or even a couch.

Anyway, back to that conception and the prayer for God to be more obvious. It took me quite a while to see, but eventually, I realized that God had answered my prayer in the form of a human being who pushed my every button and made me address every single issue I needed to work on.

Every. Single. Issue.

Well-played, Creator of the Universe. That was some serious mindfuckery. If you're clasping your rosary beads right now, calm down. Sometimes I swear at God. Not really at Him, more to Him. He can take it. What better way to work on your own issues than by having a tiny, very cute, replica of yourself that you love unconditionally when you are not quite at the point of loving yourself unconditionally.

Being Lily's mother has been one of the greatest challenges of my life. She makes me address my own issues and work on them. However, she is not a manifestation of my issues in a sweet little Buddha body. No. She is a hell-raising, fit-throwing, BIG presence in our life. She is simultaneously fiercely independent and extravagantly needy of my attention. She jumps with every ounce in her tiny body on every trigger I have. But because of how we butt heads, I have learned the most about myself and improved significantly by being her mom.

My other two children served more to fill my significantly low love tank. Chloe showed me how willing and able I was to love unconditionally and also that I was a worthy recipient of that kind of love. Peyton's easygoing demeanor and quick delight brought me absolute, complete and unadulterated joy. Lily exposed every deep flaw my years of self-helping hadn't uncovered.

Without her knowledge, she has facilitated great transformation in me as time after time I try to be the mother to her that I wanted. I fall short as often I succeed, but now I am able to say, "Hey, I messed up. Will you forgive me?"

In trying to find a better way to parent Lily that didn't involve sending her to her room for hours at a time or grounding her or taking away her toys, I found the parenting book *The Conscious Parent*, by Dr. Shefali Tsabary, and it revolutionized not only the way I parent but also the way I live.

Dr. Shefali's groundbreaking, pattern-shattering view of parenting invites parents to consider the fact that our children were not sent to us so we could fix and mold them into who we think they should be. They came here perfectly who they were designed to be in order to help us—if we can get our ego out of the way—become who we were supposed to be as well. That also means we came here perfectly, despite all of our parents' attempts to fix, mold, correct and *change* us.

Lily helps me address anger, impatience, lack of focus, and stubbornness. She has shown me how to be the person I want to be as well as how to be the mom I wanted to have and the mom I want to be. She is teaching me how not to seek approval. She has always been very happy with who she is, as I think most children naturally are before the world starts criticizing them and telling them it is not okay to be who they are, and it is *definitely* not okay to like themselves as they are.

Boys should be bigger, taller, stronger, tougher, and less emotional. Girls should be smaller, quieter, skinnier, blonder, smarter, but also athletic, ladylike, nice, and demure. The message we get loud and clear as children is that we are only okay when we are less of ourselves and more of society's standards of who we should be.

Growing up, nothing that I did seemed right in my mother's eyes. She criticized my every choice from clothing to makeup to weight to boys to parenting, but she seemed oblivious to her crazy behavior in hindsight as evidenced by this conversation: Once, before a high school dance, Chloe applied vibrant pink lipstick. Always a fan of bold lipstick, my mother said, "Oh, Chloe, you look so pretty in that bright pink lipstick! I always told your mother how pretty she looked in bright lipstick, but she never listened."

In fact, she just addressed my usually nude lips through passive aggressive comments such as, "Everyone looks better with a little lipstick on," or "I don't know what the big attraction is with lip gloss. Women need color on their lips." And once—maybe this was the compliment—she remarked on my choice of bright lipstick, "It's good to see you with some color on your lips instead of that crap you normally wear that makes you look like a corpse." I gently suggested that positive reinforcement tends to work better.

Once, I told Brad that he needed to compliment Peyton more on the baseball field. He said he didn't really think about it. He said Peyton was so naturally confident that he offered more criticism than praise because he didn't want him to get a big head. I don't know if keeping me from getting a big head was my mother's motivation for withholding compliments, but I certainly never got a big head. Instead, I grew up with a warped and distorted self-image that took me forty years and counting to let go of in order to see myself as I really am. And Brad did compliment Peyton more.

In parenting Lily, I've tried many different styles, including butting heads with her, lashing out at her, and trying to give her all the things I needed as a child because she is so much like me. Here's what I have come to realize: Butting heads doesn't work. The only conceivable way to "win" would be to break her spirit, and that would be unforgiveable. Lash out and she lashes back. Giving her what I needed as a child didn't work because despite our similarities, she is not me and did not need the same things from me that I needed from my mother. To learn this, we had to struggle through a complicated dance of my giving her things *that I needed as a child*, her rejecting them *because she didn't need them*, my feeling hurt and rejected *why wouldn't you accept this gift I gave you? Because I don't want or need it*, and then pushing her away instead of taking the time to figure out what her needs were and how to meet them.

When I am able to make these connections and break a dysfunctional pattern, she responds beautifully. She only has ten plus years of garbage to let go of compared to my forty, so she's ahead of the curve.

She still wakes up and looks in the mirror and says, "Wow, Mommy! My hair looks beautiful today!" It does. It really does. And I tell her that too.

I marveled one time that she was so pure and innocent and saw herself for who she is, beautiful and perfect without all of society's rules imposed on her. I mused, "I don't think I have ever looked at myself and thought, 'Wow, I look beautiful.'" Of course, if I had ever said that, my mom would have blasted me for vanity or conceit or egotistical behavior. If I said it now, society would likely blast me for vanity or conceit or egotistical behavior. My husband, thankfully, looks at me all the time and says, "Wow, you're beautiful."

Once, as we were discussing this with friends, Lily quietly came up behind me and began feverishly working on my hair, weaving it into a wonderful braid she created. "There you go," she said, hopping down.

I said, "Thank you, honey. What made you want to do my hair?"

She looked at me as if I were dense and missing an obvious answer, "Because you said you never felt like you look beautiful. Now you do."

Pure confidence. No doubt about it. No need for anyone's approval. There you go, now your hair is beautiful. And that's what she is teaching me.

CHAPTER 11:
REBIRTH

"We are not meant to stay wounded. We are supposed to move through our tragedies and challenges and to help each other move through the many painful episodes of our lives. By remaining stuck in the power of our wounds, we block our own transformation. We overlook the greater gifts inherent in our wounds—the strength to overcome them and the lessons that we are meant to receive through them. Wounds are the means through which we enter the hearts of other people. They are meant to teach us to become compassionate and wise."

—*Caroline Myss*

I HAVE DEVOURED SELF-HELP books and podcasts for nearly twenty years, trying to fix something that isn't broken. Trying to feel... okay? Better? Enough? Lovable? Adorable? Worthy?

There's no magic pill. No particular technique that finally puts you over the top. There are years—literal wasted years—of, "Once I have the right job or body or partner or hair or family, then I can be happy." Nothing. Not. One. Single. Solitary. Thing. Outside of you has the power to make you happy.

Read it again. Write it out and hang it on your mirror. Tattoo it somewhere on your body where you can see it every day. Nothing outside of you has the power to make you happy. You were created exactly how you are supposed to be. You were given all the tools you needed not just to survive this life but to thrive. To serve and achieve your soul's purpose.

Unfortunately, throughout your journey, one by one, comment after well-meaning comment, look after judgment-filled look, people—other wounded, messed-up people—started to pick you apart, tear you down, try to "fix" you until you could no longer remember who you were before the world told you who you were supposed to be. Before the world told you what hair or body or language or skin color or profession or sexuality was okay or normal or acceptable or God-fucking-forbid: WORTHY.

Gone were the days of lying on your back with your legs splayed out because "That's not ladylike."

Gone were the days of eating for the glorious delight and communion of it because "You'll get fat."

Gone was telling people your story, showing up and being seen for who you really were because "What will people think?"

These experiences that destroyed us were only meant to teach us. To give us varied perspectives. To help us develop compassion and empathy for a flawed world full of imperfect people. Instead, in too many instances, they paralyzed us and left us feeling insecure, not enough, and unworthy.

We don't need to learn more or better coping techniques, we need to unlearn all the faulty beliefs that are already ingrained in us because we've confused our beliefs with reality. Beliefs aren't facts, they're simply stories that we've either been told or told ourselves over and over again to the point that repetitiveness and redundancy has given them an unearned and undeserved credence.

We're not unworthy; that's a made-up story we have heard too many times. It's preposterous to believe that putting a pea under someone's mattress can determine their royal lineage, right? It's equally preposterous to believe that we will never be able to lose weight because someone told us we weren't made that way or that we don't have enough will power. It's crazy to believe that kissing a frog might turn him into a prince, but we willingly swallow the idea that we're unworthy and undeserving of love. It's as insane to believe that we are unable to succeed in a career because of what happened to us as children as it is to avoid working and cleaning our houses while we await diamond-mining dwarfs and cheerful woodland animals to perform our household chores.

Yet, too often, this is what we do. Every moment of every day that we remain stuck in cycles of judgment and condemnation, we're permitting fairytales to shape our realities. We are allowing our sweet, gentle, perfect souls to believe that they aren't enough and that we don't measure up. That we need to change, grow, shrink, fix, settle, stretch, smile, cut, or bleach ourselves to be who we are. We are living in a suspended consciousness filled with "shoulds." We are waiting to be good enough, to become who we already were, in fact, who we have always been. We don't need to do anything other than let go of all that bullshit and just be.

But we already know that, right? If we can get really quiet and block out all the noise of the world and families of origin and teachers and bosses and siblings and kids and husbands and lovers and exes, and that's a really daunting task—believe me, I know—but if we can do it, then maybe, just maybe, we can hear that still small voice that says, "You are worthy. You are lovely. You are enough. You are loved. You always have been." Maybe that voice is God. Maybe it's the Holy Spirit. Maybe it's the Universe. Maybe it's Abraham. Maybe it's the Indian food that you had last night. It doesn't matter who you believe that voice to be or what you call it; it matters only that you listen to it.

"Most things will be okay eventually, but not everything will be. Sometimes you'll put up a good fight and lose. Sometimes you'll hold on really hard and realize there is no choice but to let go. Acceptance is a small, quiet room." — Cheryl Strayed

Here's the thing: No matter how much you change, grow, regress, progress, shrink, or whatever, please hear this: THIS JOURNEY IS FOR YOU AND YOU ALONE. The people who couldn't love you at the beginning won't love you at the end. The people who thought you were an asshole will still think you're an asshole. Your mom will still criticize. Your sister will still make passive aggressive comments. The people who didn't like you in middle school, high school, college, and your kids' schools will still talk about you, and thanks to social media, you'll get to see them actively disliking you—give yourself permission to block them. You don't need their approval.

You didn't take this journey to make other people like you. You didn't, did you? Because that's not what it's about. You took this journey to heal yourself, to give yourself freedom from other people's opinions about you. You took this journey to step away from the stagnant water that's been poisoning you for too long and to tap into the fresh, clean, hydrating, nourishing resources flowing around you.

There is not one day that goes by that you can't open a book or listen to a podcast or step out in nature when you need to feel inspired and encouraged. Need someone to commiserate with you? Google Brené Brown, and you will find a wealth of empathy at your fingertips. There's no longer any reason to listen to the worn-out tape of condemnation and criticism that's played in your mind. Simply turn it off. Walk away. Walk toward the brilliant, beautiful, whole and perfect spirit that has always been inside you, waiting for you to open your eyes and your heart.

ACKNOWLEDGEMENTS

Thank you, thank you, thank you to my amazing people:

My early readers, who are dear and trusted friends: Julie Arena, Jon Swan, Julie Swan, Heidi Lateulere, Sue Mizik, Terri Yendrek, Irving Kuo, Sue Perigo, and Melissa Berry. When I trusted you with my words, I also trusted you with my heart. Thank you for the care with which you handled them.

My mother, high school and college English and writing teachers for giving me a firm grasp of the English language and how to use it properly. You've made my editors' jobs a little easier.

I am blessed to be surrounded by the most amazing network of strong, inspirational women who support and lift me and each other up: Julie, Vickie, Sue, Brandie, Lisa, Karen, Carlotta, Andrea, Tracy, Tracy, Heidi, Heather, Helene, Michelle, Trish, Christina, Carie, and Joni. I cherish you all; you're the sisters I always dreamed of.

Through their own brave writing, these amazing authors have inspired and encouraged me: Anne Lamott, Dani Shapiro, Brené Brown, Glennon Doyle, Kelly Corrigan, Marie Forleo, Rachel Hollis, Shefali Tsabary, Geneen Roth, Ann Patchett, Gretchen Rubin, Jennifer Pastiloff, Maya Angelou and Mary Karr.

Oprah, whose shows and podcast brought me to so many of the amazing ideas and authors who changed my life.

My brothers David and Richard for reading, understanding, and supporting me. And my baby sister Amy who always has my back.

My BFF, Lori, the real MacGyver, and the truest friend anyone could ask for. I'm grateful every second of every day for you. Thank you for believing in me so much that I finally started to believe in myself.

Bird, Booze, and Bugsy, I hope you know that all the work I've done was ultimately to be the best mom for you.

And Bradley: *"Yours is the light by which my spirit's born; you are my sun, my moon, and all my stars"* (E. E. Cummings).

CPSIA information can be obtained
at www.ICGtesting.com
Printed in the USA
FSHW021807200620
71391FS